"I need you, Law. I

"Help you? How?"

Raising her hands to her throat, Caroline unbuttoned her blouse until it gaped open, exposing a thin bra.

Law groaned under his breath.

Taking a step closer, she slipped the blouse off her shoulders and let it fall to the floor. "Hutch and his cult have infiltrated every part of my life. He seems to know my every movement. But he's never reached my heart. He's never been able to destroy what is between us. And I need that now. I need you."

Suddenly Law was beside her, touching her, kissing her. She felt so good. So right. As if she belonged with him. Right here, in his arms. In his bed. As if all the years and guilt and pain separating them had drifted away like storm clouds.... It would be different this time. She deserved the world. And this time he'd give it to her.

Dear Harlequin Intrigue Reader,

Summer lovin' holds not only passion, but also danger! Splash into a whirlpool of suspense with these four new titles!

Return to the desert sands of Egypt with your favorite black cat in *Familiar Oasis*, the companion title in Caroline Burnes's FEAR FAMILIAR: DESERT MYSTERIES miniseries. This time Familiar must help high-powered executive Amelia Corbet, who stumbles on an evil plot when trying to save her sister. But who will save Amelia from the dark and brooding desert dweller who is intent on capturing her for his own?

Ann Voss Peterson brings you the second installment in our powerhouse CHICAGO CONFIDENTIAL continuity. Law Davies is not only an attorney, but an undercover agent determined to rescue his one and only love from a dangerous cult—and he is *Laying Down the Law*.

Travel with bestselling author Joanna Wayne to the American South as she continues her ongoing series HIDDEN PASSIONS. In *Mystic Isle*, Kathryn Morland must trust a sexy and seemingly dangerous stranger—who is actually an undercover ex-cop!—to help her escape from the Louisiana bayou alive!

And we are so pleased to present you with a story from newcomer Kasi Blake that is as big as Texas itself! Two years widowed, Julia Keller is confronted on her Texas ranch by a lone lawman with the face of her dead beloved husband. Is he really her long-lost mate and father of her child—or an impostor? That is the question for this *Would-Be Wife*.

Enjoy all four!

Denise O'Sullivan
Associate Senior Editor
Harlequin Intrigue

LAYING DOWN THE LAW

ANN VOSS PETERSON

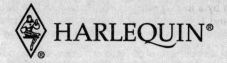

HARLEQUIN®

TORONTO • NEW YORK • LONDON
AMSTERDAM • PARIS • SYDNEY • HAMBURG
STOCKHOLM • ATHENS • TOKYO • MILAN • MADRID
PRAGUE • WARSAW • BUDAPEST • AUCKLAND

Special thanks and acknowledgment are given to Ann Voss Peterson for her contribution to the CHICAGO CONFIDENTIAL series.

ISBN 0-373-22674-8

LAYING DOWN THE LAW

Visit us at www.eHarlequin.com

Printed in U.S.A.

ABOUT THE AUTHOR

Ever since she was a little girl making her own books out of construction paper, Ann Voss Peterson wanted to write. So when it came time to choose a major at the University of Wisconsin, creative writing was her only choice. Of course, writing wasn't a *practical* choice—one needs to earn a living. So Ann found jobs ranging from proofreading legal transcripts to working with quarter horses to washing windows. But no matter how she earned her paycheck, she continued to write the type of stories that captured her heart and imagination—romantic suspense. Ann lives near Madison, Wisconsin, with her husband, her toddler son, her Border collie and her quarter horse mare.

Books by Ann Voss Peterson

HARLEQUIN INTRIGUE
579—INADMISSIBLE PASSION
618—HIS WITNESS, HER CHILD
647—ACCESSORY TO MARRIAGE
674—LAYING DOWN THE LAW

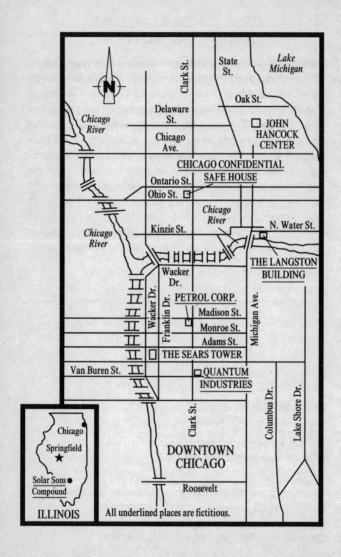

CAST OF CHARACTERS

Lawson "Law" Davies—This Chicago Confidential agent regrets many things in his life, but none more than walking away from Caroline Van Buren five years ago.

Caroline Van Buren—Kidnapped and brainwashed by a cult bent on destroying her family's business, Caroline must struggle to reclaim her thoughts and memories. But one memory is clear—the way Law Davies broke her heart.

Eugene "Hutch" Greely—The fanatical leader of the Solar Sons, Hutch wants to destroy the oil companies and return the earth to natural power. And he'll use any tool at his disposal—including murder—to accomplish his goal.

Gordon Doeller—The Quantum Industries executive had his fingers in many pies. Now he's dead. Can Caroline remember who killed him?

Natalie Van Buren—Caroline's sister will do anything to ensure her sister's safety. Even ask Law Davies for help.

Jimmy Flaherty—Caroline's assistant is dedicated to his work—and Caroline.

Sophie Wilson—Sophie has more than a simple crush on Jimmy. How far will she go to remove Caroline as a rival for Jimmy's affections?

Mrs. Hansen—Caroline's nosy neighbor knows everything that's going on. What is she hiding?

Yashi—The superintendent of Caroline's apartment building, Yashi seems to spend an inordinate amount of time in Caroline's apartment. Could he have ulterior motives?

To Denise O'Sullivan, Lynda Curnyn and
Priscilla Berthiaume for including me in this project.
And to Cassie Miles and Adrianne Lee
for making it so much fun.

Acknowledgments:

Thanks to Professor Susan Peterson for her help.

Prologue

The electronic humming rose in Caroline Van Buren's ears. It swirled around her like a physical force, beating her down, penetrating her thoughts, clinging to her skin like the smell of stale sweat. She didn't know how long she'd been in the closet. Weeks, months—forever, it seemed. It didn't matter. It was where she would be until the day Hutch Greely had promised—the day he delivered her into the arms of death.

A shiver stole over her skin. A lot had changed since she had been taken from her bed in the middle of the night by members of the Solar Sons. She'd learned things she'd never dreamed. At first she'd fought it. But she'd learned to stop fighting. And now she knew the truth. About the destruction of the earth. About her own guilt and complicity. About how much she needed to talk to people, to hear more than the incessant humming, to see the light of the sun. But one thing remained the same. She wanted to live. She would do anything to live.

The closet door opened. A shaft of light split the darkness and made her eyes blink and water. Color assaulted her. Smeared, brilliant color. She wanted to see him this time, before the closet door closed and darkness was her only companion. She rubbed her eyes and willed them to adjust.

Hutch peered down at her. Sun streamed from behind him, igniting his long, ponytailed hair into a halo of golden fire. "Caroline, it's time for us to talk."

Her heart soared at the sound of his voice. The only sound she'd heard since she'd arrived besides the lifeless humming. His hand closed around her arm and lifted her out into the room, into the sun.

She followed obediently. Legs weak and shaky, she leaned against his strength.

He led her into a dining room with maps tacked all over the walls and lowered her into one of the straight-backed chairs. Sitting on the edge of the table, he stared down on her as if peering into her soul. "You have a choice to make, Caroline. A very important choice. And I'm going to help you make it."

She'd had many discussions with Hutch in the time she'd been in the Solar Sons' prison. Discussions about the environment, about her family's oil distribution corporation, about her role in destroying the earth so her family could be rich. He'd interrogated her for hours, maybe days. Sometimes through the closed closet doors and lately more often out in the open, in the sunlight.

But never had he asked her to make a choice.

He'd made all her choices for her. He'd shown her the right answers to give—answers that would bring her rewards like the opportunity to bathe or a trip to the bathroom or an extra piece of bread to eat. He'd shown her the words to say that would prevent the hours of condemnation she'd received when she'd first come to the Solar Sons. Back when she didn't know how to think.

And now her insides quaked at the prospect of making a choice. What if her choice was wrong? Would he kill her? Would the barrage of criticism and humiliation start all over again? Would he beat her empty with her own guilt?

"Do you feel up to making this choice, Caroline?"

What could she say? She wasn't allowed to say no to Hutch. She'd learned that lesson well. And unless she wanted to be shut in the closet with no food, unless she wanted to feel the pain of his cruel words and even crueler humiliations, unless she wanted to feel that bullet he'd promised enter her brain, she'd better find the courage to come up with the correct answer. She took a deep breath and nodded. "Yes."

"Fine." He leaned forward, elbows on knees. His gaze hardened with seriousness, with intensity. "You have been doing well, Caroline. You are finally seeing the truth. The truth you have known all along."

"Yes. I can see the truth. You've shown me the truth."

"So I have. The earth needs you, Caroline. She needs you to defend her. Remember the oil spill you witnessed as a college girl? You couldn't do anything to protect the earth then, Caroline. You could only watch the black death coat the birds' feathers. You could only watch it choke the otters and drag them down into the sea. Remember?''

It had happened a long time ago, but she remembered. Too well. The only thing she didn't remember was telling Hutch about her trip to Alaska. But then, he seemed to know everything about her. Things Caroline herself didn't know. ''Yes. I remember.''

''But now you can defend the earth, Caroline. Do you want to do that?''

''Yes.'' Her mind swirled. She was so confused, she couldn't tell one thought from another anymore. But she knew she loved the earth. She cared about the environment. And that she always had. ''I've always wanted to defend the earth.''

''Yes, you have. That's why I brought you here, Caroline. You've always wanted to do the right thing. Even as you enjoyed the luxury paid for by your family's dirty oil money, the money they stole by raping the environment.''

Placing the toe of his boot on the chair seat between her legs, he leaned forward and ran a finger along her cheekbone. ''And now you have a choice to make. I am giving you an opportunity. An opportunity to live a righteous life. An opportunity to prove yourself worthy of my cause and my special friendship. An opportunity to return to your work in a lab I'll set up here at the compound. Will you join us in our fight to defend the earth? Will you join the Solar Sons and do the earth's work? Will you follow me, Caroline?''

Caroline didn't hesitate. She knew what she wanted. She wanted to do the right thing. She wanted to walk in the sun and listen to people's voices. She wanted to work again. And most of all, she wanted to live. And if she wanted those things, there was only one answer she could give. "Yes."

Chapter One

The voices in Chicago Confidential's special-operations room hushed. All eyes focused on Lawson Davies.

Oh, hell. He glanced at his Rolex. Negotiating the Chicago Loop in rush-hour traffic had been a nightmare as usual, but he'd made the trek to Solutions, Inc., a front for the Chicago Confidential office, in record time. That left only one reason for the dire looks on the faces turned toward him. Something had happened. And Law could bet he wasn't going to like it. Not one damn bit.

He focused on Vincent Romeo, the head of operations at Chicago Confidential, an elite and very covert division of the Federal Department of Public Safety. "What is it, Vincent?"

Adorned from head to toe in his usual black—including his hair, eyes and five o'clock shadow—Vincent stared at Law, his expression unchanging. In the months since Law had become an agent of the relatively new Confidential branch in Chicago, he had rarely seen Vincent's expression change. The man was always brooding, focused and intense. And this morning he certainly wasn't looking to revise his image. "Take a seat, Law."

Law scanned the faces of the others in the high-tech room. His gaze immediately landed on the only nonagent present—Natalie Van Buren, vice president of public relations at Quantum Industries, the largest buyer and seller of oil worldwide. With shoulder-length brown hair coiffed in a businesslike style, she sat in a chair at the briefing table. A nonagent was rarely allowed inside the special operations room. No doubt this briefing had something to do with the Van Buren family-owned Quantum Industries.

Law couldn't help but notice the uncharacteristically dark circles under Natalie's green eyes and the pinched lines of worry flanking her mouth. Natalie was tough. She'd recently weathered an explosion in her office, the murder of fellow Quantum executive Gordon Doeller and the hijacking of Quantum's private jet. But there had to be a limit to that toughness. What more did the poor woman have to deal with?

He looked back to Vincent. "The terrorists? Did they hit another target?"

"No," Vincent answered. "And though Zahir Haji Haleem is in custody, he still isn't talking."

The prince of a small country in the Middle East called Nurul, Zahir had hired mercenaries to hijack a Quantum jet carrying executives to a Washington, D.C. symposium. He'd even ordered the deaths of Natalie Van Buren and Chicago Confidential agent Quint Crawford when they'd tried to stand in the way of his plot. Fortunately, Quint and Natalie had thwarted the hijacking, and Zahir was captured and put safely behind American bars.

But Zahir wasn't the only one behind the plot. That much was clear. There were others waiting to carry on where he'd left off. And they suspected the head of the terrorist network was none other than the ruler of Nurul's allied country of Imad, the dangerous Sheik Khalaf Al Sayed. Chicago Confidential's only hope of ending the threat to Quantum and national security was to prove the tie between Zahir and Sheik Al Sayed and shut down their operation.

That must be what the meeting was about. Law sank into his chair at the round table behind the built-in laptop computer used for briefings. "If Zahir won't talk, where does that leave us?"

Vincent's lips quirked upward, as close as the man ever got to a smile. "We have an ace up our sleeves."

"Fill me in."

"Javid Haji Haleem has graciously agreed to take his twin brother's place. Undercover."

Law didn't try to hide his surprise. Tall, strong and infinitely intelligent, Javid, a prince in his own right, struck Law as plenty capable for the job. But it wasn't every day that the future ruler of a Middle Eastern country became a spy in order to help the United States root out terrorism. "You're telling me the prince is posing as his brother?"

"That's right. It's our best shot at infiltrating and bringing down the terrorist network. And its king-pin." Vincent's lips flattened into a line, as somber as his clothing. "But that's not why I called you here."

Law was anxious to get down to business. "Then by all means, let's get this show on the road." He looked around the room at the other agents, expecting them to take their seats so the meeting could begin.

Vincent's wife and partner in the formation of the agency, the high-born Whitney McNair Romeo, offered him a gentle smile. But she didn't move from her spot behind Natalie Van Buren. Quint Crawford, the agent who had saved Natalie's life and now was engaged to marry her, towered behind Natalie. His black Stetson clutched in his hands, Quint was all business, a serious glower replacing his usual aw-shucks grin. Even Andy Dexter was subdued. The slightly loopy telecommunications and computer forensics genius hovered over one of his high-tech machines lining the walls of the room.

"Care to fill me in?" Law asked.

Vincent gave a nod. Quint, Whitney and Andy filed out of the room, leaving only Natalie, Vincent and Law seated at the table.

Unease gripped the back of Law's neck like an icy hand. Something was going on all right. And judging from the looks of this meeting, it had something to do with him.

The moment the door closed, Vincent leveled his black stare on Law once again. "We have a situation. And judging from your experience and what Natalie has told me, you are the best man to handle it."

Law raised his eyebrows in question. He understood the part about his "experience." He'd been an attorney for the past eleven years. The first six years he'd worked in the Cook County state's attorney's office, and the past five with the oil distributor Petrol Corporation, the biggest competitor of Quantum Industries. He knew criminal and corporate law and had plenty of experience within the oil industry.

But Vincent had lost him with the comment about something Natalie told him. Natalie didn't know Law well enough to fill Vincent in on anything. At least Law didn't think she did. He'd had few business dealings with her. Even when he'd headed up Petrol's lawsuit against Quantum over a patent five years ago when he'd first came on board at Petrol, he hadn't dealt with Quantum's public relations department or the vice president in charge of public relations, Natalie Van Buren. And even when Chicago Confidential had become involved in protecting her from the recent terrorist attacks, Quint Crawford, not Law, had been assigned to Natalie.

He glanced from Vincent to Natalie and back again. "Care to elaborate?"

"It appears as though Caroline Van Buren has been kidnapped by the Solar Sons eco-cult," Vincent said.

"Caroline?" Law's heart seemed to stop in his chest. When it started again, it immediately kicked into overdrive. "I'd heard she joined the cult, but kidnapped? Are you sure?"

Natalie rose from her chair. "I've had a bad feeling about this from the first. Caroline is concerned about the environment, but I just couldn't see her joining a cult. And now I know I was right. When you see her face on the video…'' Her voice failed her, but her eyes flashed with challenge, as if ready to defend the honor of her little sister.

Vincent's earlier comment about what Natalie had told him fitted into place in Law's mind. Guilt slammed into his gut, as unforgiving as a charge of contempt from a judge's lips.

Natalie knew. She knew what had happened between Caroline and him five years ago. And she knew how badly he'd handled it afterward. She knew exactly what kind of a bastard he was. And now Vincent knew, too.

Law fought the urge to look away. Instead, he met first Natalie's and then Vincent's pointed stares. ''You mentioned a video. Do you have evidence she was kidnapped?''

Natalie nodded. ''Yes.''

''Then why don't you bring it to the police or the FBI? They're better equipped to handle this kind of case than Chicago Confidential.''

Natalie shot him a look that would have killed a lesser man. Or one with half a conscience left. ''She doesn't want to leave. She's been brainwashed.''

''Brainwashed? How can you tell?''

''I know my sister, Mr. Davies. Though obviously you don't. And never wanted to.''

She was partly right. Except for his one night with Caroline, he didn't really know her. But it wasn't because he didn't want to. It was *never* because he didn't want to.

Vincent held up a hand to stop the volley between

them. "WGN received a videotape from Caroline this morning. They are planning to air part of it tonight." He punched a button on the remote in his other hand and the high-definition video screen stretching across the room's far wall sprung to life.

Caroline Van Buren's face filled the screen. She was looking down, as if reading over a written speech one last time before delivering it. She was thinner than Law remembered. Her shoulder-length blond hair hung listlessly to her shoulders, and circles dark as bruises dug under her eyes. But there was no mistaking her face—her long eyelashes, that petite, freckle-flecked nose, and those full, lush, extraordinary lips. A pang registered in Law's chest and shot downward to his groin.

On the screen, Caroline raised her eyes to look straight into the camera.

Caroline's eyes—her brilliant blue eyes that danced and sparkled, the eyes he still saw in his dreams—had changed. Instead of shining with life and energy, they were dull, flat, emotionless. As if every bit of passion had been drained from her and all that remained was a pretty shell.

Caroline drew a deep breath and launched into her speech. "Hello. I am Caroline Van Buren. Recently my disappearance has made the newscasts along with a lot of speculation and lies. I want to clear up the falsehoods and tell you the truth.

"It has been suggested by my sister, Natalie, that I was kidnapped, but I'm here to tell you that isn't so. I thank the Solar Sons for delivering me from my own greed and sin.

"I have always wanted to defend Mother Earth. But like so many others, I was blinded by the power and money of my family and its arm of destruction, Quantum Industries. My parents gave me the best schooling and more money than I could ever spend, but in return demanded that I turn a blind eye to their sins against the earth. Well, I can't do that anymore.

"Thanks to Hutch Greely, the leader of the Solar Sons, I have changed from the selfish, greedy person I was. I've grown. I've become conscious and can never go back to the life I led before. Nor do I want to. As a result of Hutch's teachings, my love has expanded to embrace the earth. I only wish others had the courage to join me and fight for the mother who gave us all birth.

"I would like to ask my sister, Natalie, to stop spreading lies, both about my being kidnapped and about Quantum Industries. You may call your job 'public relations,' but we all know in wartime 'public relations' really means propaganda. And make no mistake, this is war. Quantum Industries is the enemy of the earth. And now it is my enemy as well. And as the vice president of evil propaganda, you are no longer my sister but my foe.

"All who would be sinners against the earth are now my enemies. I take up the scepter of the Solar Sons and I will fight to the death against your sinning ways."

The screen dissolved into static, and Vincent turned off the tape.

Law stared at the blank screen and raked a hand through his hair. Natalie was right. Caroline had been brainwashed. He flinched inwardly at the thought of her flat, dull eyes. He could picture each bitter word zinging straight from cult leader Hutch Greely's lips into Caroline's ear, to be reproduced on the video as if they were her own thoughts.

Law had seen brainwashing at its worst while prosecuting a religious-cult leader for the deaths of some of his followers back when Law was with the state's attorney's office. And the thought of Caroline—sweet, dedicated, passionate Caroline—falling victim to the kind of humiliating and abusive techniques necessary to erase free will and replace it with utter devotion made his stomach turn.

Unable to meet Natalie's tear-filled eyes, Law focused on Vincent. "The fact that Caroline now wants to be in the cult ties our hands, unless we can come up with solid evidence she's there against her will."

Vincent shook his head. "I don't want you to pursue this in the courts."

"What do you want me to do?"

"You're going to get her out."

There it was. The reason all eyes had been on him the moment he stepped into the office. Vincent had chosen Law to extricate Caroline from the Solar Sons. "And how do you propose I do that?"

"The Solar Sons are well armed, and I don't want to get into a firefight with them. So I'm sending you into the compound alone. Undercover."

"And my cover is…"

Vincent deposited the remote on his desk, picked up a sheet of paper and thrust it at Law. "You're her husband, and you want to bring your wife home."

Law looked down at the paper. A marriage license stared back at him, complete with names, dates, witnesses and his and Caroline's signatures. For a moment he couldn't speak.

Vincent filled the silence. "Natalie wanted to go, but I won't allow it."

Natalie glanced at Vincent and blew a frustrated breath through tight lips.

Vincent continued as if he hadn't noticed. "As you can tell from the video, Eugene Greely, commonly known as Hutch, has focused his efforts on turning Caroline against Natalie. Besides, we all know how dangerous the Solar Sons and Hutch Greely can be."

Natalie raised her chin, her eyes flashing with determination. "I can handle it."

Vincent looked straight at her. "After what you went through with the hijacking, I don't doubt it. But you're not a Chicago Confidential agent, and I'm not putting you in another dangerous situation. Law will handle it."

Law nodded. Although no one had been able to prove the Solar Sons were responsible for the acts of environmental terrorism their name had been connected to over the past few years, Chicago Confidential had suspected for some time they were behind many of the recent fires and small-scale bombings. And lately, their efforts to derail the oil industry and return the earth to a more natural state seemed to have hit a fever pitch.

One thing was certain, Hutch Greely was one dangerous SOB. Definitely not fit for someone like Natalie to be around.

Or someone like Caroline, either.

Law's gut clenched. "Do you really think Caroline will agree to leave with a husband she doesn't remember?"

Vincent's black eyes zeroed in for the kill. "As I understand it, there can be many aftereffects of brainwashing, including cognitive inefficiencies and short-term memory loss."

Vincent had done his homework, as usual. "Along with blunting of emotion, suggestibility and indecisiveness."

"Exactly. All of which will make it easier to convince her of the marriage. Besides, I'm counting on her remembering something of the time the two of you spent together."

Just as he'd suspected, Natalie had told Vincent about the night Law and Caroline had spent together. The night Law had unknowingly taken her virginity. The most explosively passionate night of his life.

And the last night he'd seen Caroline Van Buren.

And now he was going to use her memories of that night to manipulate her to do his will. The same way Hutch Greely was preying upon her devotion to the environment to brainwash her to do his will.

Law swallowed the bad taste in his mouth. There was no doubt about it. He really was a bastard.

LAW HAD HEARD somewhere that corn was supposed to be knee-high by the Fourth of July. But judging from the sea of cornfields surrounding this particular ribbon of highway in southern Illinois, the corn was on steroids this year. It was only mid-June and row after row of the plants would stretch at least to an average man's belt.

He could see why Greely chose to locate his commune here. The sun for which his group was named beat down unmercifully, unbroken by the shade of trees. And the monotonous flatness of the highway was enough to hypnotize any driver.

He took another gulp of now-cold coffee and forced himself to focus on the mission ahead. He wasn't sure what kind of reception he'd get at the Solar Sons compound, but he was ready for anything. He felt the weight of the .22 caliber pistol at his ankle. Even though he was dressed like a yuppie straight from the suburbs—name-brand jeans, polo shirt and athletic shoes—he wasn't about to walk into the Solar Sons compound unarmed. With a man like Hutch Greely, one couldn't be too careful. Or too prepared.

Besides, nowadays even the average yuppie might arm himself in a similar situation.

Law spotted the glint of sunlight off solar panels up ahead in the sea of corn. He swung his Jeep off the highway onto a dirt road. Dust rose and swirled behind him. Ahead an old white farmhouse and red barn rose out of the cornfield, the commonness of the setting belied by the tall fence topped with spiraled strands of razor wire encircling the area and looming over neighboring cornfields. Several rows of low buildings huddled behind the barn, each equipped with its own rooftop solar panel. As Law drove closer, he spotted acres of vegetable gardens stretched in the space between buildings.

He pulled up to the gate and climbed from his Jeep. He and Vincent had decided to start with the direct approach. Extracting Caroline with the least amount of conflict would be best. And safest. And with a man as volatile as Greely, Law was all for going the safe route. Especially with Caroline involved.

He tried to ignore the knot in his gut. This was a mission like any mission. And he would treat it as such. Get in, convince Caroline to go with him, and get out. It was that simple.

At least, he sure hoped it would be.

He strode to the gate, his athletic shoes making no noise on the soft dirt. He slipped on the wire-rimmed glasses he used for reading to complete his costume. Even as paranoid as Hutch Greely was known to be, he couldn't feel too threatened by the perfect picture of a concerned suburban husband looking for his wife.

A mountain of a man dressed in a flannel shirt hanging loose over worn jeans appeared at the gate. He looked like a kid straight out of the Seattle grunge-music scene of the nineties, except for the semiautomatic rifle clutched in his hands. "What do you want?"

"Is Caroline Van Buren here?"

The big man stared at him, obviously not feeling any compunction to answer.

"I'm her husband. I want to see her. If you don't take me to her, I'll have to return with the police."

The hulk didn't look worried. He merely turned away from the gate and disappeared into a small hut that apparently served as a guard station. When he returned, another armed hulk accompanied him. And a thin man with a scruffy beard, stringy red-gold hair pulled into a ponytail and similar attire led the way. Reaching the gate, he focused nearly colorless blue eyes on Law. There was something not right about the man's eyes. They were deep and penetrating, wild and hypnotic. His walk and the way he tilted his head to look at Law held an unsettling, kinetic quality.

A clammy chill clamped the back of Law's neck. "Hutch Greely, I presume."

Hutch only stared at him.

"My wife is in your compound. I want to see her."

"Wife? There are no wives in here. Wives are devoted to husbands. My women are devoted only to the earth."

"I want to see Caroline Van Buren Davies."

"Caroline?" He narrowed his eyes on Law. "I know all about Caroline. She isn't married."

"You obviously don't know everything, then. We were married in secret three weeks before she disappeared."

Greely didn't look as though he was buying one word. "Why the secret?"

"I work for the competition. It didn't endear me to her family. She wanted to wait to tell them."

"The competition?"

"Petrol Corporation. I'm head of the legal department."

"Petrol, huh? Every bit as corrupt and evil an operation as Quantum Industries."

If Greely thought Law was going to stand around and listen to a lecture about the evil oil industry, he'd better guess again. "Take me to my wife."

"Do you have proof of this marriage?"

Law withdrew the marriage license from his pocket and handed it to Greely. "I thought you might be skeptical."

The cult leader narrowed his eyes, studying the paper as if it contained answers to the mysteries of the universe.

"If you don't take me to her, I'm prepared to involve the authorities."

Greely handed the paper back to him and shook his head. "And what will the authorities do? Arrest the friends of the earth with no evidence? Bring them on. I'd love the publicity."

"Take me to my wife."

The smile didn't fade from Greely's face. "It doesn't matter if she's your wife or not. She's doing the earth's work now. She has purpose in her life. She doesn't want to return to her former decadent lifestyle of consumption and raping the environment."

"I'd like her to tell me that herself."

"Very well. You can see her." Hutch nodded to one of the armed men behind him. "But first, Pike will take any weapons you have."

The behemoth circled behind Law. Starting under

Law's arms, he groped him with his big mitts. He removed the Jeep's keys from Law's pocket. And then he found the ankle holster. Unsnapping it, he pulled out Law's pistol and held it in the air.

Hutch shook his head mockingly. ''Were you planning to shoot your way out of here, yuppie boy? Funny. You don't look that stupid.''

Law carefully kept all emotion from showing on his face. Without a gun or the keys to his Jeep, he was at the mercy of the Solar Sons. Or at least, that's what Greely thought. And as long as Hutch didn't believe him to be a threat, he had a chance of figuring out how to get Caroline out of this place.

Hutch walked in a circle around him, staring with those wild eyes. ''Now what should we do with you?''

''Take me to Caroline, Greely. Or are you afraid I'll point my empty ankle holster at you and run off into the cornfields with her?''

Hutch threw his head back and laughed. ''I'd love it if you did. Standard target practice is getting a bit boring for my earth brothers.''

''Then you have nothing to worry about.''

''No, I guess I don't. I'll take you to Caroline's cottage. Follow me.'' He spun on his heel and walked in the direction of the outbuildings huddled behind the farmhouse and red barn.

Law fell into step behind the cult leader. One of the armed guards stayed at the fence, while the other walked behind Law, close enough to tread on the heels of his shoes. His breath puffed in Law's ears.

Hutch led them through the middle of the compound. A military installation on the outside, the compound carried the look of a sixties commune inside. Rows of vegetable gardens tended by skeleton-thin women and children stretched between tiny clapboard cottages. Clotheslines draped with shapeless, hippie-style clothing waved in the breeze. And stylized paintings of a sun with eyes, nose and mouth decorated every shack, cottage and fence. *The Solar Sons are watching you.*

Law tried to catch the eye of some of the women and children working in the gardens. But everyone cast their eyes to the ground as Greely walked past, as if they weren't worthy to witness their leader's glory.

Law felt sick to his stomach.

Finally Hutch turned into a shack, indistinguishable from all the others, near the center of the compound. He didn't knock, but just pushed the door open and strode inside. Law and the armed guard followed.

The blonde's pencil stilled, but she didn't look up from the notes she was writing in the midst of Bunsen burners and glass beakers arranged on a scarred dining table. Her hair was as stringy as the others, and her body was draped in a dress so thin it looked like a worn rag.

"Caroline," Hutch announced. "A man is here to see you. He says he was once your husband."

She angled her head enough to peer up at Law through the drape of her hair. Her eyes focused on him, as flat and passionless as they'd appeared on videotape. "I have a husband?"

Law forced himself to nod. "Yes."

"You used to have a husband," Hutch clarified in a loud voice. "Now you have the Solar Sons. Now you have the earth as your loved one."

She dipped her head. "Yes. Now I have the earth."

Law took a step toward her and held out a hand. "I want you to come home with me, Caroline."

She raised her head, looking him full in the face. "This is my home. I don't remember a husband."

He shoved his hand into his pocket, drew out the marriage license and offered it to her. "See? We are married. Here's your signature. Remember? You belong with me."

For a moment she looked unsure. Like a little girl fighting tears. Then she glanced to Hutch and a calm came over her face. Flatness descended back into her eyes, and she shook her head. "I belong with the Solar Sons. I belong with the earth."

Hutch skewered him with a self-righteous glare. "She has made her choice. Now you'd better leave. It's a long walk to the next town." He tossed Law's car keys in the air and caught them with a jingle. Then he slipped them into his pocket and signaled the behemoth to lower his rifle on Law.

Law eyed the barrel of the semiautomatic and set his jaw. So much for the direct approach.

Chapter Two

"He was the one I've been trying to teach you to forget. The one you've had impure thoughts about. Wasn't he, Caroline?"

Caroline looked up at Hutch. He sat above her in his usual place on the edge of the table in the cabin, which had been transformed into Caroline's laboratory.

"I didn't know you were married to him. You should have told me you were married, Caroline." A thread of anger laced his voice.

Cold sweat broke out over her back and the palms of her hands. "I didn't know. I didn't remember."

Hutch raised an eyebrow. "You don't remember the man who was here? Is that what you're telling me?"

She'd recognized Lawson Davies as soon as he'd walked into her cottage—his sandy hair, his green, intelligent eyes behind wire-rimmed reading glasses, his smile that at one time seemed made just for her. She'd never forget him. "I remember him. I just don't remember marrying him. I don't remember him being my husband."

Hutch frowned. "What do you remember him being?"

A frisson of fear skittered along her nerves. She struggled to meet Hutch's eyes and searched for an answer he would find acceptable. But all she could remember about Law Davies was the heat of his bare skin pressed against hers, the flavor of his kisses, the mixture of pain and pleasure when he entered her. Heat stole up her neck and pooled in her cheeks.

Hutch's face grew dark. He slammed his fist on the table, causing the beakers to jump.

Caroline jumped, as well. Clutching her hands together in her lap, she braced herself for what she knew would come. The punishment she deserved.

"You had almost proven yourself worthy of my attentions, Caroline. But you've disappointed me."

She bent her head in front of him.

"I saved you from the others. I kept you for myself. And now when you're almost ready to move out of the closet and into my bed, you betray me by once again thinking of that other man. And not just any man, but a sinner against the earth."

"I'm sorry, Hutch."

"That's not good enough. You have to be punished. You have to purify your mind of these destructive thoughts."

Her eyes filled with tears. She'd been close, so close to being a full member of the Solar Sons. So close to being worthy of Hutch. But her thoughts of Law Davies had ruined everything. God help her, even his name filled her with memories. *Law Davies.*

"I'll do whatever you want, Hutch. Whatever it takes to purify my mind."

Hutch's face softened slightly. "I know you will. And you will start by returning to the closet until I let you out. The sight and sounds of the earth are too good for you right now." His fingers closed over her jaw and tilted her head back, forcing her to look into his eyes. "And if that doesn't clear your mind, I have a bullet in my rifle that will."

LAW EYED THE ROLL of razor wire along the top of the compound's fence. The brutal barbs caught the moonlight, sparkling like a strand of Christmas lights. He had heavy-duty wire cutters in his Jeep that would take care of that wire with a few snips. Unfortunately his Jeep was now on the wrong side of the wire. He would have to find another way.

He would do anything to get Caroline out of that place. And after seeing the deadness in her eyes—eyes that he remembered flashing with such vitality, such passion—he couldn't shake the feeling that he'd better get her out tonight.

He eyed the tall fence again. He wasn't going over the fence, not with that razor wire at the top. And he could rule out going around or through. That left only one option.

Hunkering down in the waist-high corn, he crawled to the fence's foot. Thanks to the corn, the guards could see him only if they faced him dead-on. From the side, he was hidden.

He thrust his bare hands into the earth near the fence. The tilled dirt moved easily. He scooped handful after handful away from the base of the fence. As long as the fence didn't extend too deeply into the ground, he had it made. But he had to hurry. He had a lot of digging to do. And though many hours of darkness stretched ahead, the night wouldn't last forever.

Beads of sweat gathered on his back and forehead as he worked. His fingers hit the bottom of the fence wire, and he dug into the harder ground on the other side. His fingers ached. His hands were becoming raw. He found a sturdy stick and used it to break up the hard-packed dirt.

Guards circled the perimeter fence twice, forcing him to abandon his digging and withdraw into the cornstalks. But eventually he had a ditch dug under the fence, hopefully just deep enough for him to squeeze under. He glanced at his watch. He still had a couple hours of darkness. And he'd need every minute.

Lying down on his back, he pushed with his legs. His back grated along dirt. Inch by inch, he slid his body under the wire. Reaching the other side of the fence, he scrambled to his feet and ducked into the hulking shadow of a nearby solar panel.

He scanned the compound. Dark shapes of cottages sprang up everywhere, like trees in a forest. He had to find the right cottage.

He located the little guardhouse next to the front gate and struggled to get his bearings. Counting the number of cottages they'd passed when Greely had led him to Caroline this afternoon, he spotted the cottage. With any luck, he could duck into the cottage, grab Caroline, and duck back out through the ditch under the fence before any of the Solar Sons were the wiser. It was a tall order, but one he had to accomplish. His odds weren't likely to get better with the passage of time. And he simply couldn't leave her here one more day.

At least he wore a blue shirt, not a color that would catch the moonlight and make him a moving target. He should be able to make it.

Drawing a deep breath, he crouched low and ran across the open expanse to the next cottage. Keeping his eye on his destination, he ran from the shadow of one cottage to the next.

Finally, he reached the cottage where he'd seen Caroline this afternoon. A steady electronic hum rose from inside, audible even through the closed door. He grasped the tarnished doorknob. Holding his breath, he turned it. It moved easily under his fingers. He pushed the door open and slipped inside.

The cottage was dark. He took a moment to let his eyes adjust to the moonlight filtering through the dingy windows. As he had noticed earlier in the day, the cottage comprised a single room, void of furniture except for the long dining-room table that served as a makeshift laboratory. He locked the door and stepped farther into the room until he could see the outline of maps and charts posted on the walls. Colored pins marked areas of the map and glittered like jewels in the moonlight stretching through the windows. This cabin served as a laboratory and some sort of war room.

He searched through the papers on the table and

the maps on the walls. A bad feeling crept over his skin. Even though Hutch had referred to this cabin as Caroline's cabin, except for the makeshift lab, there didn't seem to be any trace of her.

Damn. He'd have to start peeking in the windows of the cabins closest to this one and hope he found her before the Solar Sons found him.

He raked a hand through his hair. He couldn't think with that humming in his ears. Then he heard a single thump. He looked in the direction of the sound. A radio sat on the floor near a closet door, apparently tuned to some sort of test band. A large padlock fastened the metal hasps of the closet door.

He could have sworn the thump came from that locked closet. He crossed the room and leaned his ear against the door. No sound reached him but the hum from the radio. Still, he couldn't shake off the heavy feeling that clutched his lungs. He wanted a look in that closet.

He sized up the lock. He'd never be able to open it. But judging from the simple thick steel pins holding the hinges in place, maybe he didn't have to.

Glancing around the room, he spotted a steel ruler positioned below one of the maps. He grabbed the ruler and returned to the closet door. Fitting the edge of the ruler under one of the hinge pins, he pried until the pin started to slide from the hinge. After loosening the lower pin in the same manner, he slipped both pins out and lifted the door off its hinges.

Huddled on the floor of the tiny dark closet, hands

over her ears, Caroline looked up at him with unsee-
ing eyes.

Heart lodging in his throat, he fell to his knees
beside her and gathered her in his arms.

She clung to him like a frightened kitten, her body
trembling.

He smoothed his hand over her hair. "Caroline.
It's Law. I've come to get you out of here."

She pulled back from him. Her eyes latched onto
his face and focused. "Law?"

"I'm going to take you home. Everything is going
to be okay."

"Home?" She stared at him, her blue eyes glowing in the faint light. She shook her head, slowly at
first, then gaining force. "No."

Law reached for the belt around his waist. "It's
okay, Caroline. I'm here. You're safe."

She kept shaking her head. "You're a sinner
against the earth. My mind has to be purified."

"It's okay. I'm going to take you home to your
family."

"This is my home. The Solar Sons are my family."

He slipped his belt free and wrapped it around her
wrists, tying them in front of her.

She didn't struggle, merely watched him, eyes
wide, as if nothing she could do would prevent the
horror that he was perpetrating against her.

He felt sick, but he had no choice. She clearly was
not going to go with him voluntarily. Her wrists secure, he pulled his shirt off over his head.

Her eyes widened even farther at the sight of his

naked chest. A gurgle sounded from deep in her throat. She tried to wrench away from him.

He swung a leg over her and straddled her thrashing body, holding her still between his thighs. Hurriedly, he twisted the shirt in his hands. He had to get the blasted thing in her mouth. He could feel the scream building inside her. He held the shirt to her mouth, trying to ease it inside without bruising her lips.

A squawk erupted from her throat. It grew to a scream, ripping through the air just as he slipped the shirt between her teeth.

Her scream died. She stared up at him as if he was going to kill her. A whimper rattled from her throat. Her chest rose and fell with labored breaths.

"I'm not going to hurt you, Caroline," he whispered in her ear. "I promise I'll never hurt you."

She stared as though she didn't hear him. Or didn't believe a word he said.

He swung his leg off her.

The moment she was free, she kicked out at him, her foot falling short of the mark.

He tried to lift her to her feet.

She refused to stand, hanging in his arms like a limp doll.

"Please, Caroline. You have to cooperate. I'm your husband. Remember? I'm saving you. I'm going to take care of you."

She twisted in his arms, trying to knee him in the groin.

He dodged the strike. This wasn't working. It wasn't working at all. Even over the infernal humming, he could hear movement and the shouts of voices outside the cottage. The cult members must have heard Caroline's scream. Soon he and Caroline would have company. He had to get her out of the cottage if they were going to have any chance of escaping the compound.

He turned her so her back pressed against his chest. Circling her with his arms, he held her tight.

She thrashed, struggling to break free.

He held on. He pressed his head against hers, his mouth next to her ear. "Hutch is going to be angry, Caroline. He's going to be angry with you because I'm here."

She shook her head, but stopped thrashing as if paralyzed with fear.

He may not be able to gain her cooperation, but at least she'd stopped fighting him so hard. That's all he needed. Lifting her from her feet, he carried her to the nearest window just as the first blow landed against the locked door.

Chapter Three

Caroline shook with fear. Numbness stole over her body. She had to fight. She had to escape from Law. Hutch or his men were at the door. They would help her. They would save her. She only had to fight. But try as she might, her body wouldn't move.

Another thump landed against the door.

Law set her on her feet next to the window. Turning her to face him, he unlocked the sash and swung it open. He placed his hands on her waist. The muscles in his bare chest tensed, preparing to lift her.

She bit down on the shirt he'd slipped into her mouth—the shirt that smelled like Law.

Another blow sounded against the wood. The door was sturdy, but it would crack soon. It would fly open and Hutch and her earth brothers would rush inside. They would help her. They would save her.

She couldn't let Law drag her away from the Solar Sons. It was the only place she belonged. Summoning all her strength, she kicked Law's shin. Her bare foot connected, but he didn't even flinch. She tried to wrench herself away from his grasp, but it was no use.

Law lifted her as if she weighed less than a doll and thrust her feet through the open window. He dropped her on the ground outside and climbed through after her. As soon as his feet hit the ground, he grabbed her elbow and raced across the middle of a vegetable garden, pulling her in his wake.

Just as they ducked into the shadow of the neighboring cottage, Caroline heard another loud thump followed by the crack of wood. Her earth brothers had broken the door down. They were inside the cottage. Soon they would see the empty closet. They would know she was gone. They would search for her.

Law started for the next cottage, dragging her along behind him.

Circling the last cottage, Law stopped dead. Following his gaze, Caroline spotted a pile of dirt on the other side of the fence and a narrow ditch under the wire. Two of her earth brothers stood near the hole, moonlight glowing dully off the barrels of their rifles.

"Damn, damn, damn," Law ground out through clenched teeth.

Caroline slumped against the wall of the cottage. She struggled to breathe around the shirt in her mouth. It was over. Hutch would find her soon. He would make everything all right.

Doubt fought through the confusion in her mind. Was Law right? Would Hutch be angry? Had her own impure thoughts about Law brought this on? ·

She pushed the thought away. Hutch would do the

right thing. He would save her in spite of herself. All she had to do was let him.

But before she could brace herself against Law, he was moving again. She followed, her bare feet sinking in the soft garden soil. He pulled her through gardens and around cottages and past the barn, until the front gate loomed into view. Law stopped and ducked into the farmhouse's shadow, dragging Caroline with him.

A single earth brother guarded the front gate. He walked the length of the gate, turned and walked back again. Caroline braced herself against Law's shoulder. The guard seemed so far away, like she was peering at him through the wrong side of a microscope. Small as a pinhead.

Law said something to her, but she couldn't hear the words. She just stood there watching the guard, all emotion, all thought extinguished. As if she was back in the closet when the horror all fell away and she was left outside of her mind.

She felt herself moving again, pulled by Law. They ran toward the guardhouse and ducked inside before her earth brother completed his lap of the fence and turned to face them.

Crouching on the floor, Law rummaged through the shelves in the guardhouse. He grasped a two-way radio and a long metal bar. Then he tucked her into a corner of the little shelter and crouched in the doorway, scrutinizing the earth brother's movements.

As she watched Law, her mind started to clear. Her sight returned to normal. She should yell, warn her earth brother. But she couldn't speak around the shirt in her mouth. Couldn't move. Couldn't breathe. Couldn't feel. She watched, as detached as if she'd walked into a movie halfway through and couldn't care less what happened to the characters.

Law waited until the earth brother turned his back and headed the other way along the fence before he slipped from the guardhouse and tossed the radio over the earth brother's head.

It landed with a clatter against the fence. The earth brother turned his weapon on the sound. Law sprang close behind him and brought the length of iron bar down on the brother's head. He collapsed into the dirt.

Law raced back to the guardhouse. Punching the button that unlocked the gate, he grabbed Caroline by the arm and pulled her to her feet.

She followed him out of the guardhouse toward the open gate. She stared down at her earth brother's still form as she passed. The man groaned and tried to lift his head. He was hurt. She had to help him. She had to stop. But Law didn't hesitate. He pulled her out the gate.

Just as they cleared the fence, shouting exploded from behind them. Hutch and the others. A gun cracked. Bullets whizzed over their heads.

Hutch's promises rushed through her mind. Promises of punishment. Promises of a bullet in her brain. He'd seen her with Law. He thought she'd betrayed him. And for that, she would surely die.

LAW DIVED into the corn. He twisted, pulling Caroline down on top of him to break her fall.

She landed partially on his chest. Her eyes searched his, their clear blue depths filled with pure terror. Her nostrils flared with labored breaths.

He had to convince her to go with him willingly. If he didn't, they were both dead. "Caroline, listen to me. I'm going to untie you and take the gag from your mouth. But before I do that, I want to know if you're with me."

She stared at him as if he was speaking another language. Her eyes were glazed, confused.

"Hutch is very angry. Do you hear the gunshots? He's trying to kill you. You have to escape from him now. Will you do that? If I untie you, will you let me help you escape?"

The gunshots and shouts of Hutch's men drew closer.

She jerked her head in the direction of the sounds. Eyes wide with fear, she nodded.

"Good." Reaching around the back of her head, he untied the shirt he'd jammed in her mouth as a gag.

She scooped breath after breath into her lungs. Her hands were still tied by the belt. He fumbled the belt free. She'd need her hands for crawling through the corn. Speed was the most important thing now. The small head start they had on the Solar Sons and the maze of corn were the only things they had going for them. "We have to crawl. Keep your head down."

She stared at him, her face pale and eyes sharp.

"You first. I'll follow. Move as fast as you can."

She nodded, but didn't move.

"Now would be a good time."

She started as if just awakened from a nightmare. Scrambling to her hands and knees, she began crawling. Her flimsy dress reached only to midthigh, leaving her legs bare. But she scrambled over the clumps of dirt without flinching, cornstalks rising on either side.

Law followed. He could hear her labored breathing even above his own.

Shots sprayed the cornfield in isolated bursts. A spotlight swept over the corn.

Law hit the dirt, a rock digging into his cheek. "Get down."

Caroline collapsed, flat against the ground.

Damn, if he only had his pistol. If he could return fire they could get out of here. As it was, they could only crawl and hope a bullet or the spotlight didn't catch one of them. "Caroline. Lie still until the light passes."

The beam moved over them. The leaves of the corn glowed neon green. The stalks' shadows lengthened, but still cloaked them, shielding them from the glare. Law held his breath. Finally the light passed over and moved on to search another area of the field. Law climbed back to his knees. But Caroline still lay facedown in front of him, not moving. "Okay, Caroline. Crawl."

She lifted her upper body with trembling arms and then fell back to the dirt.

"Damn." Concern shot through him. He scrambled alongside her.

She lay with her cheek on the dirt, staring at him,

breathing hard. Tears trickled down her cheeks and soaked into the dust. "I—I'm sorry."

"You have no reason to be sorry." He should have thought of her lack of physical strength and conditioning before he put his damn fool plan into motion. For God's sake, she was nothing but skin and bones.

Law ground his teeth until they ached. He could easily guess what Greely had done to her to coerce her into believing every radical word from his lips. No food. No sleep. No exercise. Sensory deprivation. Endless interrogation sessions. Maybe even hypnosis. Add the constant fear of death, and it was no wonder Caroline was spouting Solar Sons' rhetoric and was weaker than a child. Trained soldiers had succumbed to less. What Law wouldn't give to close his hands around Greely's neck and squeeze the life out of the son of a bitch.

Law drew a deep breath and smoothed a blond strand off her cheek. "You're going to have to climb on my back and hold on. Can you do that?"

She swallowed hard. "I think so."

"Good." Law lay facedown on the ground next to her. "Now climb on my back and wrap your arms around my neck."

She did as he ordered. Her thin arms circled his neck and locked in a tight embrace. Her hair draped over his shoulder and tickled his skin.

Memory surged through him. Memories of her slim, toned body pressed against him. Five years ago she'd had stamina and passion to spare. More passion than he'd ever known.

He forced the image from his mind. He could think of only one thing right now. And that was saving Caroline's life. And saving his own.

He hoisted himself to his hands and knees and resumed crawling. Clumps of dirt bit into his hands, already sore from digging under the fence. His knees scrambled through the dirt. And Caroline clung to him, the soft caress of her breath in his ear.

He had no idea how long he crawled, but the shouts eventually faded behind them, and the gunshots grew fewer and farther between. It was a big field for Hutch and his followers to cover, no matter how many "earth soldiers" he had in his Solar Sons army. But Greely would eventually catch up to them. Unless they found a way to get the hell out of there.

Up ahead, a light danced between the leaves of corn. Had Greely's men circled them? Were he and Caroline surrounded? He stopped. The light stopped dancing, as well.

Law blew a relieved breath through tense lips. The light was stationary, positioned high on a pole in the middle of a farmyard. The white hulk of a barn glowed through the shadows of trees. He lowered his head and crawled as fast as he could toward the light. If he could reach the farm, he could borrow a vehicle or call the other Chicago Confidential agents for help.

He pushed himself to crawl faster. His hands were numb now, past feeling, but his knees had begun to throb.

Finally he reached the edge of the field. The house and barn loomed in front of him. And the voices had grown louder behind. Greely and his Solar Sons were catching up.

"Grab my shoulders, Caroline."

She did.

He rose upright on his knees and grasped her legs, wrapping them around his waist. "Hold on. I'm going to make a run for it."

Her fingers dug into his shoulders, and she craned her neck in the direction of the cornfield. Obviously she, too, heard the voices growing closer.

He struggled to his feet and sprang into a dead run. He raced across the sloped farmyard and straight for the house. Reaching the door, he slammed his fist on the wood, the thunder of his knock reverberating through the house.

He listened hard for any sound from the house. Footsteps. A voice. Nothing.

A click sounded near his ear. A rifle being cocked. "Don't move."

Law's heart froze. Caroline whimpered deep in her throat.

"Let me see your hands."

Law released Caroline's legs and held his arms out at his sides. Caroline slipped to the ground behind him, her body still pressed against his. He could feel her tremble as she raised her hands.

"What the hell are you doing on my property?"

"Your property?" Law released the breath he was holding with a whoosh.

"Damn straight, my property. Are you two from that hippie cult? What the hell were you doing out there? Shooting up my corn?"

"I called the sheriff's office," a woman's voice yelled from inside the house.

"Good," the farmer said from behind them. "They'll take care of this."

The sheriff's office. Law could only hope the deputies got here quickly. Before the Solar Sons reached the farm. Even now he could hear their shouts growing closer. He doubted the farmer's single deer rifle would be much of a match against the Solar Sons' arsenal.

"What's this on your wrists?"

Law glanced over his shoulder to see what the farmer was referring to.

Caroline held out her arms. Purple bruises bloomed around her wrists.

Law's gut hitched. Had his belt done that?

The farmer scrutinized her arms in the farm's yard light. "My God. Were you tied up, honey?"

Caroline said nothing, just stared at her wrists as if they belonged to someone else.

Law twisted around, trying to look the farmer in the eye. "I'm her husband. I rescued her from the cult."

The farmer looked down at Caroline's bare feet and flimsy dress then focused narrowed eyes on Law. He tightened his grip on the rifle. "Rescue? Looks more like kidnapping than rescue to me."

The scream of a siren cut the air. Two county sheriff's cars snaked around curves and pulled into the farm's short driveway. They moved into position. One deputy approached. "I have them, Earl. You can put the rifle down."

The farmer lowered his deer rifle. "He kidnapped her out of the cult on the other side of my cornfield."

The deputy moved up behind them. "Kidnapping, eh?"

Law could see the nod of the farmer's head shadowed on the farmhouse siding. Damn. If only he could tell the deputy he was a federal agent. But he couldn't risk the farmer overhearing him. Or worse yet, Greely. "I was rescuing my wife from the cult. She's with me voluntarily. I'm taking her home. You heard the shooting. The cult members were trying to kill us both."

The farmer shook his head. "I've lived next to that cult for two years now. I don't like them much, but I've never had any trouble with them shooting up my corn before. Sure haven't heard of them taking anyone against their will."

The shouting in the distance had stopped. The predawn air was still except for a few birds testing their early-morning voices. An uneasy feeling crept up Law's spine. The Solar Sons weren't looking for them anymore. They'd found them.

The deputy eyed Caroline. "What about it, ma'am? Did this man force you to leave the cult, or did you leave of your own free will?"

Caroline's eyes darted to the barn hulking in the shadows. The same shadows that hid Hutch Greely and his followers. Hutch, who was listening to every word from her lips. She drew in a sharp breath.

Law flinched. He had no idea what she would say. Especially with Hutch close enough to hear her answer. And if she said the wrong thing, he could end up in jail, and she back in Hutch Greely's cruel arms. And Hutch might even be angry enough to kill her.

"Well, ma'am? Is your husband taking you home or kidnapping you?"

Law held his breath.

Caroline pulled her gaze from the barn and focused emotionless eyes on the deputy. "I want to go home."

Chapter Four

Caroline turned her face to the shower's spigot and let hot water sluice over her, washing all traces of shampoo, sweat and cornfield dust down the drain. She hadn't taken a hot shower since Hutch had come for her, weeks—no, months ago. She'd missed the way the water cascaded over her skin, its heat soaking into her bones.

Reaching through the stream, she turned off the water. Hutch had warned her about the tactics the enemies would use to seduce an earth soldier to the side of decadence and greed. First a bounty of food—homemade chicken soup, crusty bread and a ripe, juicy peach in her case. Then the hot shower. No doubt chic clothing and a soft bed would follow.

She drew in a breath of humidity and set her chin. She'd spent too many years of her life being deceived by her family's money and privilege. She couldn't let herself fall back into that sinful way of life. Not now that Hutch had opened her eyes.

Guilt seeped into her like a chill, penetrating her bones and leaving her shivering. She'd been so confused when her earth brothers had started shooting at her. So frightened. She hadn't known what to do. Law had offered her a way out. A way to save her life. And God help her, she'd taken it.

In doing so, she'd betrayed Hutch and the Solar Sons. She'd betrayed her calling to defend the earth. She was weak, impure, a traitor. No wonder Hutch had wanted to kill her.

She turned off the water and wiped moisture from her eyes. There was only one thing she could do now. She had to get away from Law and the sinners of the earth. She had to return to the Solar Sons. She had to beg Hutch to take her back to the only place she belonged.

She stepped out of the shower and dried herself with a thick terry-cloth towel. Her dress was gone, whisked away by the woman Law had charged with taking care of her. Instead, a pile of folded clothing perched on the vanity. A pair of black leggings and an oversize Chicago Cubs T-shirt. Not chic, but comfortable. Her clothing from another life. She dressed, leaving her feet bare.

Knuckles rapped on wood. "Are you decent in there?" A female voice with a soft New England accent filtered into the steamy bathroom.

Caroline smoothed strands of damp hair back from her face. It was time to confront the enemy again. To stand up to the next temptation they offered. To figure out some way to redeem herself in Hutch's eyes and return to the Solar Sons. She pulled open the door.

The woman named Whitney stood outside. Beautiful with her well-styled, red-gold hair and designer clothing, she looked like a poster child for sinners-of-the-earth excess. "You look human again. It's amazing what a good meal and a hot shower will do for the spirit."

Caroline didn't return Whitney's smile. The woman's painted lips and seemingly sincere gray eyes didn't fool her any more than the meal or hot shower. "I want to leave."

"I'm sorry, Caroline. That's not possible."

Caroline should have known. She was a prisoner. Her prison may offer a cornucopia of food and hot running water, but it was a prison just the same.

Whitney moved her slender body to the side and gestured into the adjoining room. "Come into the sitting room. You'll be more comfortable out here than in that steamy bathroom."

Caroline stepped from the bathroom and walked in the direction of Whitney's extended arm. A sitting room opened in front of her, separated from the bedroom by a wall of glass block. A floor-to-ceiling window stretched along one outside wall, the view shrouded by miniblinds. Two chairs huddled around a small table bearing a lamp and a vase of fresh-cut flowers.

Caroline passed the chairs and walked to the window. Splitting the blinds with her fingers, she peered outside. Between the neighboring buildings, she could see a sliver of the John Hancock Building stabbing into the sky. Judging from the view, she was near North Michigan Avenue. The Magnificent Mile. One of the nation's centers of greed and excess. A world away from the Solar Sons compound.

"Do you like flowers? I thought it would be a nice touch. A woman's bedroom should always have flowers in it."

Caroline looked at the tender blossoms of Japanese iris, freesia and baby's breath. "They should be growing in swamps and fields the way nature intended. Not dead in a vase."

Whitney's smile faded. "We're here to help you, Caroline."

"You're here to turn me against the earth."

Whitney shook her head. "Lawson wanted to talk to you as soon as you were out of the shower. I'll tell him you're ready to see him."

Lawson. Law Davies. Images clustered in the back of her mind. His heat, his scent, the feel of his solid body against hers. A shiver slunk up her spine. She pushed the images away. The impure thoughts. She had to be strong. Only if she was strong might she be able to get back into Hutch's good graces. "I don't want to see Law."

Whitney flashed her a polite smile. "You don't have a choice in the matter." Turning, she disappeared down the hall, leaving Caroline in the room alone.

Caroline let the blind slats fall closed and lowered herself into one of the chairs. Clenching her hands in her lap, she studied her stubby fingernails.

When she'd run from the Solar Sons compound, she'd been afraid. Afraid of the Solar Sons' bullets. Afraid of Hutch's wrath when he found out what she'd done. But now, among the enemy, she felt numb. No fear. No anger. And certainly no happiness. Nothing at all.

She tried to think of her marriage to Law, but no images materialized. All she could remember was the taste of Law's kiss, the press of his body pinning her against a wall, the hot surge of pleasure and pain when they joined.

She had to purge her mind of such thoughts. She had to find a way to return to Hutch.

"I trust Whitney took good care of you." Law Davies's voice rumbled from the doorway.

She raised her gaze to meet his.

He peered down at her from the entrance to the sitting room. A fresh white shirt stretched across his chest, and his hair gleamed like a sandy beach bathed in sunlight. His eyes seemed to look into her, through her, penetrating as green lasers.

Caroline tangled her fingers together in her lap and held on. Talking to Law was dangerous. He made her feel something, a shiver of awareness or a tinge of warmth. His mere presence conjured up images she'd be better off to forget. Impure images. Carnal images. And most dangerous of all, the rumble of his voice, the sincerity in his eyes made her want to believe every word from his lips. And if there was anything Hutch had taught her, it was not to believe sinners of the earth. "I want to go back to the Solar Sons."

He exhaled in a whoosh, as if her request had knocked the breath from his lungs. "You can't do that, Caroline."

"Am I in a prison?"

"You're in a safe house. Hutch wants to kill you. We can protect you here."

"No. He was only shooting at me because he thought I went with you willingly. If I can explain to him that—"

"No, Caroline. It's too late for that. Hutch Greely is a dangerous man. He won't give you a second chance."

"You're wrong. You have to be wrong. Hutch has to give me a second chance. I have to return to the Solar Sons compound. It's the only place I belong."

Law watched her, silent. But she could guess what he was thinking.

"I know you say you're my husband. But I don't remember anything about our marriage. I've changed. I've grown. And the Solar Sons have helped me do that. They've made me a better person. I have to return."

"We aren't married."

"What?"

"You don't remember our marriage because we were never married."

An electric shock jolted through her. "You lied?"

"Yes."

She shouldn't have been so surprised. Hutch had told her sinners of the earth lied. That they wielded money and luxury like weapons. That they used people and threw them away like trash along a country road. But somewhere deep inside she had the idea Law was different. Or more likely, she'd just wanted him to be different. "Why did you lie?"

"It was the only way to convince Greely to let me see you."

His voice was so flat, so matter-of-fact that she wanted to hit him. To hurt him. To pound her fist against his chest until he was bruised and battered. "Do you realize what you did? Hutch and the Solar Sons are my life. You took away my life."

"Greely is not your life. You had a real life, a full life, here in Chicago. You had your work, your family. Hutch stole all of that from you. I just brought you home."

He didn't get it. He didn't get it at all. "My life is with the Solar Sons."

"You don't understand, Caroline. You can't go back. If Hutch finds you, he'll kill you."

She cradled her head in her hands. Despair clogged the back of her throat. "No, you don't understand. If I can't go back, then I might as well be dead."

LAW RAKED a hand through his hair. Damn. Greely had done a number on Caroline, all right. He'd taken away her free will, her power of independent thought. But not only that, he'd taken away her life and her reason for living it.

He had to make Caroline see the truth about Greely. And he would. Even if it killed him. "I'm sorry for lying to you, Caroline. I'm sorry for causing you pain. But I'm sure as hell not sorry for rescuing you from that damn closet. And I'm not going to apologize for getting you out from beneath that bastard Greely's thumb."

Caroline's lips drew into a bloodless line. She leaned back in her chair, her face drawn, her eyes fixed in an empty stare. "Hutch is a great leader."

"A great leader, Caroline? His men weren't shooting blanks at us when we escaped through the cornfield. Those were real bullets. He was trying to kill us, Caroline. He was trying to kill *you*."

"That's your fault, not Hutch's. Before you came, he was trying to save me." She shook her head and looked him in the eye. Her blue eyes were dull, void of feeling. A look that cut him deeper than self-righteous anger or a flood of tears ever could. "And you tricked me into going with you. Hutch told me sinners against the earth lie. If I'd had a pure mind, I would have listened to him."

"He locked you in a closet. He brainwashed you. Hutch is the one who lied to you."

She looked at him as if he were a dense child. "Hutch doesn't lie. He's a great leader. He fights to save the earth."

"He kidnapped you."

"He didn't kidnap me. He saved me."

"What did he save you from?"

"My family. Quantum Industries. Greed and lies."

She was spouting the same rhetoric she'd used in her speech on the videotape. All he could hope to do was keep poking holes in that rhetoric until she could finally see the Solar Sons for what they were.

Easier said than done. "You were doing work that will help the earth when Hutch 'saved' you. You developed a hydrogen-combustion engine. You were working on a formula to split hydrogen from water and stabilize it to fuel that engine. Hutch stopped your work. How does that help the earth?''

''I'm still working on the formula.''

He thought of the makeshift laboratory she'd been in when he'd first seen her at the compound. ''With a Bunsen burner and a couple of beakers? That's a far cry from your lab at the Quantum building.''

''Quantum wanted to squash the research. They wanted to hide it away to protect their oil profits.''

''What makes you think that?''

''Hutch told me.''

''If Quantum wanted to bury the hydrogen-combustion engine project, why did they pour all that money into your research in the first place?''

''To fool me. To fool the world. They wanted the world to believe they were doing something good for the environment, but really they were protecting their oil profits. It was all Natalie's idea. What she calls public relations.'' Caroline looked him dead in the eye, her face drawn and blank as a robot reciting the programming fed into it. She sat back in her chair and crossed her arms over her chest.

So much for that line of questioning. He wouldn't get anywhere with her on the subject of her family. ''So what happens to your work now? Do you just play with the little toy lab set that Hutch bought you?''

''Hutch will get me a full lab when I'm worthy to continue the earth's work.''

''Worthy? When will you be worthy?''

''When I can purify my mind.''

''Purify your mind of what?''

She focused on the carpet. "I've worked so hard to improve my thinking. I've done so much to prove myself to him. I've done everything he's asked. And now you've ruined it all."

Everything he's asked? Law gritted his teeth. He knew the standard operating procedure of some cults, the practice of passing women around, the leader taking first choice. That was how the cult he'd prosecuted had worked. He could just imagine what Greely asked, and it had little to do with beakers and Bunsen burners. "How have you proven yourself?"

"I am a soldier for the earth." A defiant tone echoed in her voice. "I do what I have to."

Did that include sharing Greely's bed? He tightened his fists until his hands ached. Just the thought of Greely touching Caroline's satin skin made him want to hit something. Or someone. Preferably Greely himself. "What has he asked you to do?" The words came out on a growl.

"I can't say."

"Why not? Hutch's work is righteous, isn't it?"

"Yes. Hutch is righteous. He fights for the earth."

"Then why keep his work a secret? His work could inspire millions to fight as well."

She narrowed her eyes to blue slits. "You're trying to trick me."

"I just want you to tell the truth, Caroline. There should be no problem with telling the truth. You said Greely speaks the truth. So why do you want to hide the truth from others? From me?"

"I don't want to hide the truth."

"Then tell me what he has asked you to do."

Dropping her gaze to the floor, she gripped the chair arms as if hanging on for dear life.

"If Greely is all that is good and right, you shouldn't be ashamed."

She raised her chin, but still didn't meet his gaze. "I'm not ashamed."

"Then why don't you tell me?"

"I—" She stammered, then clamped her lips together.

"You are ashamed, aren't you? Hutch isn't as righteous as he wants you to believe. He took advantage of you."

"No."

"He is just using the earth's cause to feed his own needs."

"No. Hutch cares about the earth more than anything."

Law didn't doubt it. Though Hutch was fanatical, Law was sure the man truly believed in his cause. Just as he believed kidnapping, brainwashing and destruction was justified to advance that cause. And, no doubt, that a great leader deserved some spoils. Perhaps *that* was his weakness. The weakness Law could use to get Caroline to see who Hutch really was. "The Solar Sons give Greely everything he needs. A comfortable living. Followers who will do anything he wants. Sex with any woman he chooses. No wonder he cares so much about the earth."

"It's not like that."

"No? Then why won't you tell me what he asked you to do? Why don't you tell me the truth?"

She writhed in her chair. "He asked me to prove myself."

"How?"

"He didn't say how. I had to choose how."

Law's stomach rolled. Greely had even had the gall to make what he'd ordered her to do seem like her choice. The bastard made him sick. "So how did you prove yourself, Caroline? What did you do?" He braced himself for her answer.

She swallowed hard and raised emotionless blue eyes to meet his gaze. "I killed a man."

He nearly choked. He had expected her to say many things, shocking things, but this wasn't one of them. "You what?"

"I killed Gordon Doeller."

Chapter Five

"Impossible. It's impossible." Law muttered under his breath to no one in particular.

Sitting in front of one of the computers lining the walls of Chicago Confidential's special operations room, Andy Dexter raised his blond mop top from his work. "What's impossible?"

Law hit another key on his computer, switching the screen to display the next page of the report detailing Gordon Doeller's murder.

A photo came on the screen. A late-model luxury sport utility vehicle hulked, charred and blackened like a burned-out house. Visible inside the vehicle, the shape of a human head rested against the headrest.

Law adjusted his reading glasses before switching to the next gruesome crime scene photo. A close-up of Doeller's wrists bound by some sort of natural fiber filled the screen. The fiber was charred beyond visual recognition. "It's impossible for Caroline Van Buren to be responsible for Gordon Doeller's death."

"Gordon Doeller. You mean the vice president at

Quantum Industries who was toasted to a crispy crunch in his SUV?''

Andy had such a way with words. It was a good thing Vincent usually kept him chained to his computers and didn't let him out in the world. The quirky genius would need his own public relations firm to smooth over his social gaffes and crude comments. ''Yes, that's the Gordon Doeller I'm talking about.''

''Didn't the autopsy and analysis show that he was doused with gasoline and burned alive?''

Law nodded and switched to another photo. A close-up of Doeller's face, the charred skin shrink-wrapped to the man's skull in a gruesome mask of horror.

''What a way to go.'' Andy chuckled and shook his head. ''What makes you think Caroline Van Buren did it?''

''I don't. But she insists she killed him.'' No matter what kind of brainwashing Hutch had subjected Caroline to, Law couldn't believe she would douse a man with gasoline, strike a match and listen to the agony of his screams. It was impossible. Besides, Doeller was killed only a couple of weeks after Caroline vanished in March. She couldn't have gone through the rigorous months of brainwashing yet when the murder occurred.

After he'd recovered from the shock of her admission, he'd tried to push her for more details of Doeller's death. But she had just repeated that she'd killed the man. Seeing that the questioning was going nowhere, he'd convinced her to lie down, waited until she was sound asleep and then, leaving her under

Whitney's capable guard, he'd gone straight to the Solutions, Inc. office. He needed to learn more about Doeller's death if he was going to ferret out the truth behind Caroline's admission. If he could throw detailed questions at her, she would have to give him more detailed answers. And maybe she'd be forced to throw off the Solar Sons' rhetoric and think for herself. Maybe she'd tell him the whole truth.

The door slid open. Vincent Romeo and Quint Crawford strode into the special-operations room. Raised voices erupted from the lobby beyond.

Law shot Vincent a furrowed-brow look. "What's going on out there?"

Quint answered for Vincent. "Kathy is having another knock-down-drag-out with that pretty boy, Liam Wallace, who does maintenance."

Law raised an eyebrow at Quint. "So what are Kathy and Liam arguing about this time?"

"They're locking horns over which football team is going to be better this fall, the Chicago Bears or the Green Bay Packers." Quint hooked his thumbs in his pockets and rocked back on the heels of his boots. "Waste of time. Any fool can see my Cowboys have the NFC all sewn up."

Law shook his head. He'd learned months ago not to talk football with Quint. The man was a Texan through and through, which meant there was no reasoning with him.

Andy pushed his chair back from the computer and stood. "I need some coffee. Anybody else?" Not even waiting for an answer, the whiz kid scampered for the door.

Law watched him go. At least the kid had learned to ask if he could bring coffee back. The next step was teaching him to wait for an answer.

Law returned to his own work. But he'd hardly started when Vincent walked up behind him and stopped. Spinning around in his chair, Law turned his attention to the head of Chicago Confidential.

Vincent's eyes bore a hole right through him. "How is Caroline Van Buren?"

"Hostile, confused." Law explained Caroline's confession.

Vincent's gaze moved over the laptop screen. "And you're sure she didn't have anything to do with Doeller's death?"

"I've heard plenty of confessions—real and false. And Caroline's confession was as false as they come. She couldn't supply any details of Doeller's murder."

"Couldn't that be attributed to her confusion and faulty short-term memory?"

Law had considered that possibility for about three seconds. "I don't see it. I think it's more likely Hutch used the glitches in her memory to convince her she committed the murder in the first place."

Quint shuffled his cowboy boots on the low-napped carpeting. "Do you think she was there? Witnessed the murder? Is trying to protect the person who did it?"

"Maybe. But I think Greely told her she did it, over and over again, and that's the only thing she remembers clearly."

Vincent bobbed his head in a single, decisive nod. "Well, she's not your problem anymore."

Law snatched his glasses off his face and narrowed his eyes on Vincent. "What do you mean, she's not my problem?"

"Our role in this is over. The family will take care of her from here on out."

Law jumped to his feet. "The family? They can't handle this situation. Hutch Greely is not going to just give up and go away. He's probably in Lake Forest right now, staking out the Van Buren mansion."

Vincent nodded, unfazed. "I warned them that would be the case, and Henry Van Buren has hired extra security."

"And she needs help to overcome the brainwashing."

"Henry has flown in Dr. Phillip Bradshaw from Princeton."

Law knew Bradshaw. Hell, everyone did. He was one of the foremost psychiatrists in the country, a widely acknowledged expert on the effects of coercive persuasion and thought reform. Law had consulted with him on the cult case he'd prosecuted while with the state's attorney's office. Caroline couldn't be in better hands.

Then why couldn't he shake the pressure assaulting the back of his neck? "It's common for people recovering from something like this not to trust doctors, and Greely did a damn good job of turning her against her family. If they take her back to Lake Forest, she'll be surrounded by people she thinks of as the enemy.''

Vincent crooked a black eyebrow. "You're protesting pretty strongly for a man who didn't want this assignment in the first place."

It was true. He *didn't* want this assignment. Hell, he didn't want it now. He didn't want to be anywhere near Caroline Van Buren. He didn't want to see her empty blue eyes—eyes he remembered brimming with passion. He didn't want to smell the delicate musk of her skin or dream about kissing those extraordinary lips.

But he also couldn't abandon her. Not this time. "Things have changed since two days ago. I'm close to getting through to her. I can help her. *And* I can keep her safe. I can't just walk away."

"Maybe you can help her. Maybe you even should. But Caroline Van Buren isn't Chicago Confidential business anymore. She has a family. A family very willing and able to care for her. And we have bomb-happy terrorists on our hands, if you'll remember. I need you to concentrate on that."

Law searched his mind for an argument to sway Vincent. "But what about Gordon Doeller? If the Solar Sons killed him, who knows what else they could have done. We already know Greely is targeting the oil industry."

"So you will continue to look into the Solar Sons' activities. And Caroline Van Buren will return to her family home."

"Caroline is probably a witness to Doeller's murder, Vincent. Who knows what else she saw at that compound.''

Vincent screwed his forehead into one of his trademark glowers. ''I thought you said Greely kept her locked in a closet. How much could she have seen?''

''Her cottage at the compound also served as some sort of war room where Greely planned his activities. There were maps on the walls, pushpins marking the location of each office complex both Quantum Industries and Petrol Corporation have all over the world. Caroline could know a great deal.''

Vincent blew a breath through tense lips.

Quint pulled out a chair and parked a cowboy boot on the leather seat. Leaning elbow on knee, he looked Vincent in the eye. ''Seems to me, the man has a point. We don't want to lose control of a witness.''

Vincent looked from Law to Quint and back again. ''I seem to be outnumbered here. You win. You stick with Caroline. But I want you to be careful.''

Law patted the Glock tucked in the shoulder holster under his arm. ''Hutch Greely won't get near her.''

''Greely is only one concern.''

Vincent didn't have to say more. His meaning was crystal clear. And if Law had any doubts, Quint's uncharacteristically pointed looks would have cleared them up right away.

Don't take advantage of Caroline again.

Little did they know, he didn't need the warning. He may have acted like a selfish bastard five years ago, but he wouldn't take advantage of Caroline now.

He couldn't. Because he could never live with himself if he hurt her again.

CAROLINE OPENED her eyes. The ethereal scent of freshly laundered sheets teased her nose. A white, down comforter billowed like a cloud at the foot of the bed. And the bed she slept on was so soft, it seemed her body was floating.

She didn't belong here.

Her dreams hadn't reflected the heavenly nature of her surroundings. No, they'd been filled with the smell of burned human flesh, the sound of bloodcurdling screams and the tinny taste of fear. Physically she may be in heaven, but her mind was mired in hell.

She needed Hutch to make sense of it for her. She needed him to tell her what to think. She'd get out of this prison and find her way back to Hutch. She'd throw herself at his mercy, beg for his forgiveness. It was her only chance.

Throwing back the covers, she rifled herself out of bed. A pair of tennis shoes lay near the arched doorway leading to the sitting room. She slipped them on and tied the laces. Passing the bathroom, she tiptoed to the door and leaned her ear against the wood.

No sound reached her. She twisted the knob. The door was unlocked and it pulled open easily. She stepped into the hall and walked down the plush carpeting to the stairs. She couldn't detect a single sound from downstairs, either. Was she alone in the safe house? She couldn't be, could she?

She crept down the stairs to the kitchen level. It

was deserted, as well. One flight lower, she glanced around a pristine living room. There were only a few steps left and she'd be out the front door. She had no idea how she'd get out of the city once she escaped the town house, but she couldn't think of that now. She couldn't think of anything but getting back to the shelter of the Solar Sons before Hutch became too angry with her. Before he refused to take her back.

She scampered down the stairs to the front door. Unlocking the dead bolt, she pulled the door open.

"Ducking out for a breath of fresh air?"

Caroline turned toward the familiar voice.

Law Davies stood behind her in the entryway. He leaned against the banister, his ankles crossed as if he'd been relaxing in that very place for hours. How long he'd been watching her, she didn't know.

For a moment she wanted to go to him. Fall into his arms and let him take care of her. But she couldn't give in to those impure feelings, those memories of how solid his body felt, how warm his embrace. "I want to leave. I want to return to the Solar Sons."

Law's forehead creased with obvious concern. And something else. Something hard and determined. Something that made her pulse throb in her ears. He looked her straight in the eye, as if he could see into her mind. "We need to talk."

She forced herself to return his gaze. She didn't have to say much, and she didn't have to listen. All she had to do was pretend she was cooperating, pretend she was listening. She'd get this over with, and then she'd find an opportunity to escape. "Okay. If you want to talk, then talk."

Law's fingers closed around her upper arm. He guided her to the steps and lowered her to the plush carpet. He sat on the step next to her.

Caroline drew a deep breath and concentrated on the solid feel of the staircase under her, the scent of shampoo in her freshly washed hair, the way the light reflected off the cut-glass insert in the door. Anything but the man sitting next to her. Anything but his questions.

He leaned toward her, his eyes boring into her. "I have been looking at the police reports concerning Gordon Doeller's death."

A yoke of guilt settled over her shoulders. She didn't want to think of Doeller. She didn't want to think about what she'd had to do to protect Mother Earth. But she wasn't going to deny it. Not now that he knew. She shot Law a steely look. "Gordon Doeller was an enemy of the earth. His death was a casualty of war."

"You didn't kill Doeller, Caroline."

An electric shock traveled up her spine. She shook her head. "You're lying to me again."

"No, I'm not, Caroline. Not this time. You didn't kill Doeller."

"I can smell his flesh burn. I can hear his screams."

"You may have been there. But you didn't kill him."

"I killed him. I proved myself to Hutch. I belong in the grace of the Solar Sons. You're trying to trick me."

"Then tell me how you did it. Take me through the murder, step by step. How did you kill Gordon Doeller? How did you prove yourself?"

"I burned him."

"Step by step. How did you detain him in his vehicle?"

Confusion washed over her. She fought to keep her vision from narrowing, her mind from floating away. "He was in the seat. He couldn't get out."

"Why not?"

She groped through her mind for an answer. Finally grasping something, an image captured like a snapshot in her mind. "He wore his seat belt."

"Why didn't he just unhook it and climb out? You must have used something to restrain him."

She tried to think. She could see something wide binding his hands. Not rope. Something soft and wide, like the seat belt, but not. "Something. I don't know. You're confusing me."

"Did you have a gun?"

A gun. She didn't remember ever touching a gun in her life. "I don't know. I must have."

"Did you use some sort of accelerant? Paint thinner? Dry-cleaning fluid?"

Again she groped through the darkness in her mind for an answer. This time she recalled a smell. An unmistakable smell. "Gasoline. I used gasoline."

She could tell by the slight fall of Law's shoulders that she had come up with the correct answer. She looked straight into Law's green eyes.

A mistake. A shiver peppered her skin. Another

memory trying to break free. Another feeling. This one having to do with peering into Law's eyes, touching his skin, kissing his lips. She shoved it away.

"What did you do next?"

"I…" Her mind wouldn't work. She must have done something, but she couldn't think of what.

Law kept looking at her in that intense way. As if he was peering inside her and seeing all her secrets laid bare. "How did you set him on fire? Did you use a cigarette lighter?"

She couldn't remember. She couldn't think. She leaped on his suggestion. "A lighter. Yes, I set him on fire with a cigarette lighter."

"Or did you use a match to start the fire?"

"I…" What did she do? She couldn't remember. She couldn't remember so many things. "I killed Gordon Doeller," she stated again, the only thing she was really sure of.

"You don't remember how you killed him because you didn't kill him, Caroline. You were obviously there. You may have even seen who did kill him. But it wasn't you."

"It had to be me. Hutch said I did it to prove I was worthy. He said it was a step in the right direction. He said once I purged the impure memories from my mind, I would be a true member of the Solar Sons. Then I could move out of the closet and into his bed."

Law's hands flexed into hard fists. "What impure memories did he want you to purge, Caroline?"

Warmth traveled up her neck and flushed her

cheeks. The memories again surged behind her eyes. The feel of Law's lips. The scent of his skin. No. She couldn't let such things fill her head.

"You don't remember how you restrained Doeller in the SUV. You don't remember if you used a match or a lighter to set him on fire. You don't remember any of the things you would remember if you'd killed him. Were those the memories Hutch wanted you to purge from your mind? Did he want you to forget you killed Doeller?"

"No. I confessed to killing Gordon Doeller every day."

Law's gaze grew dark. "Did he want you to forget that you *didn't* kill Doeller?"

"No. I killed him."

"Hutch lied to you, Caroline. He set you up to take the fall for a murder you didn't commit."

"No. No. No." She shook her head so hard, her hair felt like whips lashing against her cheeks. "Hutch doesn't lie. Hutch's words are the truth."

"Then what memories did he want you to purge? What did he want you to forget?"

Thunder rose in her ears. Words burst from her mouth. "He wanted me to forget the man I had been involved with. He wanted me to forget *you*."

Law's expression froze. He stared at her as if she'd just sucker punched him.

Memories surged at the back of Caroline's eyes. She pressed her fingers to her eyelids, trying to push the memories away.

"Caroline." Law's voice slipped past the colors

mushrooming behind her closed lids. Rich and warm like melted chocolate, it wrapped around her mind. "What about me did he want you to forget?"

"The night we were together." She opened her eyes and drew a deep breath. Now that the words had started, she couldn't stop them. She couldn't push them back. "When you came to the compound and I saw you again, I remembered it was you I was with once. I remembered the heat of your skin, the taste of your kiss. Hutch said I had to stay in the closet again. Until I was worthy to experience the sights and sounds of the earth. Until I was worthy of him."

Law's lips tensed into a rigid line. "I'm sorry, Caroline. That night shouldn't have happened in the first place."

"I'm not sorry." She gripped the edge of the stair to keep herself from spinning away.

Law looked at her. His lips were poised to speak, but no sound came from them.

Blood rushed to her face. She didn't want to forget his kiss. His touch. The hot press of him as he entered her and filled her so completely. She wanted to remember all of it. To lock it away in a secret place in her heart. "Hutch wanted me to be sorry, but I couldn't do it. I couldn't forget."

Her mind shattered, shards whirling around her. The things Hutch taught her. The memories of her life before. Feelings she'd had at one time but couldn't feel now. She buried her face in her hands.

Silence hung in the air. Finally Law sucked in a long breath, as if he'd surfaced after being submerged for a long time. "And you never killed Gordon Doeller, did you, Caroline?"

She tried to think. She tried to remember. She tried to sort the truth from the lies. "It happened after I'd been in the compound only a little while. I'm not sure exactly how long. The air was cold. Sometime in the spring, I think. I don't remember." She shook her head. Her mind wouldn't function. She didn't know what was a true memory and what was a false one.

"Go on, you're doing fine."

"I was so cold, I couldn't stop shaking. Gordon's face seemed to glow white like a ghost in the night. He begged for his life." She tried to take a deep breath, but pressure tightened around her ribs. She shook her head again. The image wouldn't go away. "I was there."

"But you didn't kill him."

"I remember his screams. I remember the smell." A shudder wracked her body. "I remember Hutch telling me I killed him."

"But you don't remember killing him yourself."

She struggled to clear her mind, to think. She didn't remember how she tied Doeller's hands and feet. She didn't remember how she started the fire. She didn't remember killing him. She only remembered Hutch telling her she did. Making her repeat the words. Making her confess to the murder every day before she was allowed to eat, to sleep, to work. "Hutch lied to me."

"Yes."

Tears spilled from Caroline's eyes and rolled

down her cheeks. Tears for the truth she'd lost sight of for so long. Tears for the lies that had crumbled away. And mostly tears for the unknown she now faced. Because if it was true, if Hutch had lied, if everything she believed in was gone, then where did that leave her?

Chapter Six

Law reached for Caroline and enfolded her in his arms, guiding her head to rest against his chest. Sobs shook her body. Tears soaked into his shirt and dampened his skin.

"It's all right. You're going to be all right." He brushed his lips over her forehead, over her cheeks. The salt of her tears mingled with the sweet flavor of her skin. He smoothed a hand over the blond silk of her hair and felt the sobs wrack her frame.

He was here to help Caroline, to help her sort through the jumble of lies in her mind, to help her remember and think for herself. And most of all, he was here to protect her. But God help him, the press of her body against his chest, the scent of her hair, the taste of her skin—all of it threatened to sweep him away like a gushing river. Like it had five years ago.

It didn't help that she remembered—that she *wanted* to remember—their night together. The way their passion had ignited while grinding to the music of a gritty blues guitar. The way Law had looked into her eyes and knew he had to have a taste of that life, that passion. The way he hadn't been able to wait for a soft bed, but had taken her against the wall as soon as they closed her apartment door.

And the way that afterward, she'd admitted to Law's shock that she was a virgin.

Guilt twisted low in his gut. He'd played those memories over and over in his mind. And his behavior seemed more reprehensible with each replay.

He withdrew his arms from around her, his fingers from her hair. As reprehensible as Hutch Greely was, he was right about one thing. Caroline would be better off if she could purge the memories of that night from her mind.

If only Law could as well.

Caroline stared straight ahead, tears winding down her face and pooling under her chin. She wrapped her arms around herself and held on tight. "Law?" Her voice was so soft, at first he couldn't be sure he'd heard it.

"Yes?"

"What else did Hutch lie about?"

"A lot of things. Your family, for one."

"I saw a letter…a memo…I don't know what it was. But it was addressed to my father from Natalie. It outlined the plan to bury my research, Law. I'm not imagining that. I don't think I'm imagining it." A moan rose from her lips and she buried her face in her hands.

He reached out to pat her on the shoulder, but withdrew his hand before he touched her. If he touched her, he'd only want to take her in his arms again. And he couldn't let himself do that. "It must have been something Hutch wrote, Caroline. I know your family. I don't think they would do something like that.''

''I don't know them. I don't know what they would do. I don't know anything anymore.'' Her voice was muffled in her hands.

''It's okay.''

''How can you say that? I don't know how to think. I don't know how to feel. I don't know if I *can* feel.''

''That will pass with time.''

''Will it?'' She let her hands fall from her face and land in her lap. ''And what will take its place this time? If I don't believe Hutch, who do I believe?''

''You'll think for yourself, Caroline. I know it's hard now. It's damn near impossible. You've been through a horrible ordeal. But it will pass. You'll learn to trust your own thoughts and feelings again.''

''What *are* my thoughts and feelings? Who am I? I don't even know who *I* am anymore.'' She closed her eyes. She looked so lost, as if she had no friends, no family. As if she was all alone in the world. ''Someone burned a man to death right in front of me, and I don't even remember who did it. I can't feel anything but guilt and fear. I can't even say what's a lie and what's the truth. I don't know who to believe. I don't know if I can trust anyone at all.''

''You'll adjust. It will just take time.'' He knew his words sounded lame. Hell, they were lame. No help at all. But he didn't know what else to say.

Vincent had been right. Law should have turned

Caroline over to her family. To the people who loved her. To the doctor who could help her. God knew, he wasn't helping. He shouldn't be anywhere near her.

She angled her body to face him. Raising her gaze, she searched his face as if desperate to find something to hold on to. "Will you tell me the truth?"

He swallowed hard. The truth. He owed her that much. "Yes."

"Did you use me that night five years ago?"

"No. That night was a mistake, pure and simple."

She shivered, as if his words had chilled her to the bone.

He probably sounded cold to her, but what else could he say? "Rely on your family, Caroline. They love you. They'll get you the best doctors. Doctors who will help you sort through your feelings. Doctors who will help you reclaim your life."

A bitter smile tweaked the corners of her lips. "I can't trust my family. And I'm not going to trust some doctor."

"Do you trust Greely?"

"No. Not anymore."

He blew a relieved breath through tight lips. At least he had helped her see Greely's true colors. If nothing else, he'd done that.

"I don't trust anyone. But I do know one thing."

"What's that?"

"While everyone has lied to me, you're the only one who did it for my own good."

"A dubious distinction."

"Maybe." She reached out and took his hand in

hers. Her touch was desperate. Needy. And he felt his fingers tighten around hers with an answering need. "You haven't always been honest, but you're being brutally honest now. Even when the truth makes you look bad."

"The truth has a way of doing that."

"And I believe you'll tell me the truth from here on out."

He had no choice. He'd seen enough betrayal, enough disappointment when he looked into her eyes. He damn well didn't want to be the cause of any more.

"Will you help me get my life back, Law?"

He drew in the sight of her, the scent of her, the softness of her hand in his. He shouldn't be anywhere near her. He'd disappointed her before. What was to keep him from doing it again? But looking into her eyes, hearing the note of need in her voice, he couldn't turn away. "Yes. I'll help you. You can rely on me."

LATE THE NEXT MORNING, Caroline followed Law up the steps to her second-floor apartment. She could negotiate these stairs in her sleep. She remembered doing that very thing countless nights after working late in one of her Quantum Industries labs.

It had been Law's idea to bring her back to her home. He'd thought the familiar surroundings would help her connect with her old life.

Though the day was sunny and comfortably warm, she wrapped her light jacket tighter around her shoulders. Her old life seemed as though it had happened so long ago, she didn't know if she'd ever connect with the woman she had once been. She just hoped this trip into the past would help her to fill some of the holes in her memory. And help her *feel* something again—something she knew was real.

Something beyond confusion and fear.

Law reached the landing and turned to wait for her to catch up. "Your apartment was checked before we arrived. It's safe."

Once she'd reached the landing, she turned to look at the short-napped carpeting covering the stairs and the small, tastefully decorated lobby below. So far, the building felt as familiar as the grinning cowboy standing at the foot of the stairs. "Who is he?"

Law shifted his weight from one foot to another as if he was uncomfortable with the question. "A man I work with."

"He's from Petrol Corporation?"

"He doesn't have anything to do with Petrol. He works with me at another place. A little moonlighting I do."

"Hey, Ms. Van Buren," a man's voice called from down the hall.

She turned away from the cowboy and in the direction of the voice. A short, swarthy man with a heavy accent waved a screwdriver at her in an odd version of a salute. A tool belt slung low around his waist, so loaded with equipment it was a wonder he could stand upright under the weight. A grin so large it had to be forced to spread over his lips. "Happy to see you back."

She nodded in response. The man looked familiar,

but for a moment she couldn't place him. She bit her bottom lip, digging through her memory for a hint.

She could feel Law watching her struggle. Finally he showed her a little mercy. ''The superintendent of your building.''

She slipped that piece into the puzzle in her mind. Another piece followed. She remembered him. He'd started working in the building last year, maybe around Halloween time. Though she almost didn't recognize him without the gray wool cardigan he'd worn like a uniform through the long Chicago winter. ''Yashi. His name is Yashi.''

''Very good.''

She started toward the super and the door to her apartment. ''Yashi, it's nice to see you.'' The words came out on a shaky breath, but at least they came out. A normal greeting, like countless others she must have extended in her former life.

Though it didn't seem possible, his smile grew wider. ''I'm changing your lock. I will leave a key.''

She didn't remember asking anyone to change her locks. She glanced at Law.

''I asked him to.''

The door across the hall jutted open. An older woman with hair the color of burned cherries poked her head out the door. ''I see you're working on Caroline's apartment again, Yashi. How about my garbage disposal? Do I have to dye my hair blond and drop twenty years before you'll fix anything in *my* apartment?''

Yashi's smile faded, and he turned back to the door lock without comment.

"Well?" the woman said, voice shrill. Finally getting no answer, she turned to Caroline, her eyes cold. "Hello, Caroline."

"Mrs. Hansen." Caroline drew in a sharp breath. The name had popped out from nowhere. Details about her neighbor followed in a rush. "How is your cat doing?"

The woman's manner softened. "Prissy's fine. Thank you for asking." Her gaze landed on Law. She crooked a plucked-and-penciled eyebrow.

The last thing Caroline wanted to do was explain who Law was to her neighbor. She forced a smile to her lips that she didn't feel. "I'm glad."

"You haven't been around much lately."

Apparently, Mrs. Hansen had missed the videotape Law had told her had aired on WGN. Caroline searched her mind for an excuse for her absence. She came up empty.

"She's been spending a lot of time with me," Law supplied.

Mrs. Hansen narrowed her eyes. "And who are you?"

"Lawson Davies." He held out his hand.

After a limp shake, Mrs. Hansen dismissed him and skewered Yashi with her gaze once again. "She hasn't even been around and you still take better care of her apartment than you do of mine."

Yashi seemed to shrink under the shrill voice.

Caroline positioned herself between Mrs. Hansen and her target. "I'm sorry for keeping Yashi so busy. I'll try not to take up so much of his time."

The woman focused on Yashi. "Remember, I hear

you every time you walk down this hallway. So no more trips to Caroline's apartment until my garbage disposal is fixed.''

"Yes, Mrs. Hansen,'' Yashi said. The tension drawing the muscles of his shoulders tight was clear.

An uncomfortable feeling brushed over Caroline's skin. She hadn't been here for weeks, maybe months. Why was Yashi going into her apartment when she wasn't home?

Law gestured to her apartment door. "Shall we, Caroline?''

She slipped inside the door. Law followed. As soon as they moved out of earshot of the door, Law faced her. "You seemed to remember Mrs. Hansen all right. That's a good start.''

She had remembered. Strange. "I don't know how. She and I did favors for one another occasionally, but I was never close with her. I don't think I liked her much.'' She shifted uncomfortably at the sound of her own words. They seemed to be coming from someone else.

"I don't blame you. She's a piece of work.'' Law paused, his forehead creasing in thought. "Does she always hear everything that's going on in this building?''

Caroline nodded as more details of her former life came back. "She has the hearing of a wolf. I can't tell you how many times she's complained about my alarm clock being too loud. The volume's so low it doesn't wake me, yet she hears it.''

The furrow between Law's eyebrows dug deeper. "Strange.''

She wasn't following. "Why?"

"It's strange she didn't hear anything when the Solar Sons kidnapped you."

"How do you know she didn't?"

"After your parents got word that you might have joined the Solar Sons, they had a private investigator check up on you. He interviewed Mrs. Hansen. She swore she didn't have any idea where you'd gone."

Caroline's stomach contracted into a cold knot. So her parents had checked up on her. Maybe they did care. Or maybe her father was just concerned about her patent and her ongoing research. Hutch had said they wanted to find her.

"What do you remember about the kidnapping?"

She struggled to sort through her mind. "I went to one of the Solar Sons' demonstrations at the capitol in Springfield. I'd been following their work for a while. I agreed with much of what they said. But I just couldn't condone their tactics. I met Hutch at that rally. That was the last I heard of them until several months later."

"When he kidnapped you?"

"Yes. A night in March. There were three men, I think. Yes. Three men came that night. Hutch and two others. When I first saw their shadows leaning over my bed, I screamed." She had been so frightened her heart had seemed as if it would pound through her chest.

How could Hutch have made her believe those men had rescued her?

"So Mrs. Hansen should have heard something."

"Yes." Her head throbbed. She struggled to slow

the tempo of her breathing. "So what does that mean? Did Mrs. Hansen help Hutch kidnap me? Why would she do something like that?"

Law laid a calming hand on her shoulder. "I don't know, Caroline. She might not have anything to do with it. But either way, we'll find out."

His touch sent waves of heat through her body. She drew in a deep breath. Her mind was in chaos, and with Law's touch, her body was lapsing into chaos as well. She had to get a handle on her memories, her emotions. She had to think straight. She stepped out from under his hand and across the gleaming parquet floor of the entryway. "I'm ready to have a look around now."

For a moment, Law's gaze hovered on the wall just inside the apartment door, then he gave her a sharp nod. "Lead the way."

She walked past the spotless white-and-stainless-steel kitchen and into the living room. Familiar cream walls stared back at her, unmarred with nail holes or artwork of any kind. She raked her gaze over white leather furniture and glass tables that looked as if they'd never been used. It was a pretty room, but cold. Lonely. Dust hung in the air and covered everything with a layer of neglect.

She walked to the patio door, which opened onto a small wrought-iron balcony. Lincoln Park opened before her like an explosion of nature. All around the park's lush green oasis, the city moved. Jumbled. Alive.

And she could feel none of it.

Caroline moved through the room and down the

hallway to the bedroom. Surely there would be something more personal there. Something to raise memories. Something to spark emotion.

Law followed her, his footsteps barely audible on the lush carpet.

She pushed open the bedroom door and stepped inside. The same empty cream walls greeted her. A four-poster bed loomed in the room's center. A photo of her family perched on a white dresser and a framed picture of Wrigley Field hung on one wall.

She walked to the dresser. Picking up the family photo, she searched the faces, trying to sort her memories from the stories Hutch had told her. Caroline's father's broad shoulders took up most of the picture, his personality exuding from his smile like a physical force. Hutch had called him brutish, dishonest, greedy. Was he really like that? She couldn't say.

A smile spread over her mother's lips, its passivity belied by the flash of Irish humor and temper in her eyes. Hutch had little to say about her mother. He'd only claimed she liked the good life Quantum had brought their family. Caroline supposed that was true enough. Mother liked nice clothing, her beautiful home, her life of charity events and business socializing. But most of all, she wanted the happiness of her family. At least that was the woman Caroline thought she knew.

Pulling her gaze from her mother, she focused on Natalie. Her older sister sat regal and composed in the foreground of the photo, refined and perfect and oh, so professional. Hutch had said Natalie was ambitious. That she'd do anything for the company. And the more Caroline searched her memory, the more she was convinced he was right. She and Natalie had been close growing up, but their different work paths had separated them long ago. Caroline was pretty sure they talked now and then before Hutch had taken her into the Solar Sons, but she didn't remember them connecting for a long time. Not really.

Finally Caroline forced her eyes to move to the final family member in the photo. Herself. Hutch had said many things about her. He'd described her guilt, her greediness, and finally her redemption—if only she'd follow him. She looked into her own eyes, bracing herself for a flash of recognition, a strong sense of identity and emotion to seize her throat.

Nothing happened. It was as if she were looking at a stranger. Someone she had never met. Reasonably attractive, lips a little too big for her face, sparkling blue eyes. The freckled girl next door.

She turned back to Law and shook her head. "This isn't working. I feel like I'm in a stranger's home."

He frowned as if he was hoping even more than she was that she would experience some kind of breakthrough on their little tour.

She set the family photo back on the dresser. Next to the photo lay a metal button. Remnants of soft gray wool clung to the button, as if it had been ripped from the garment to which it belonged. She ran a finger across the raised red cross on the recessed blue background. The flag of Iceland. A memory niggled in the back of her mind. Natalie. Natalie had a wool sweater with buttons like this one. A gift from the Icelandic branch of Quantum Industries.

But there had been no sweater for Caroline. No one gave research scientists sweaters.

It wasn't much of a memory, but it was a start. She picked up the button and slipped it into the pocket of her jacket. She'd look at it later, maybe more memories, more feelings about her sister would come with time.

She turned her back to the dresser. The tour hadn't been a total waste of time. She had some memories of this place. Living here *alone.* Rattling around this perfect apartment with its unblemished walls and unstained furniture *alone.* Sleeping *alone.*

She looked back at the bed. A light green comforter stretched over the breadth of it, perfect and unmarred. Save for a note card propped against the pillows. A note card fashioned in the shape of a sun and staring at her with embossed eyes.

Memories and emotions ricocheted through her mind like bullets. Hutch's promises rang in her ears, clear as they had been the endless days he'd uttered them. Promises of death and damnation if she didn't follow him. And she could almost see him looking down on her, the light behind him transforming his long, cinched mane into a flaming aurora of righteous hatred.

Law followed Caroline's gaze, spotting the card, the eyes staring out of the yellow sun. *The Solar Sons are watching you.* Anger flared in his gut. "Damn Greely."

Caroline didn't move. She didn't blink.

He pushed past her and leaned over the bed. Using the edge of a pillowcase to prevent smudging any prints that might be on the paper, he opened the card, expecting a threat, expecting some damn message about defending the earth. The inside was blank. But the card itself was message enough.

He turned back to Caroline. She still hadn't moved. Her breathing was shallow, her eyes fixed and blank. As if she was in some kind of trance.

Damn. She was dissociating. She was escaping from the sight of the sun by separating her mind from reality. A skill she no doubt perfected while trying to survive in that damn closet.

He grasped her arm and shook her gently. "Caroline. Feel the pressure of my fingers on your arm. Focus on my face. Concentrate." He shook her again.

Slowly the spark of life returned to her eyes. A flush of color moved up her neck and settled in her cheeks.

Still holding on to her arm, Law guided her out of the bedroom and down the hall to the dining room. Once there, he lowered her into a chair and squatted, facing her.

"He was here. He—" Her voice cracked.

Law let his gaze roam over her face. "He's not here now. Stay with me. You're safe." If only he could do something to comfort her. He longed to take her in his arms, to smooth his fingers over the freckles dotting her nose like spots on a fawn, to kiss those extraordinary lips until she forgot all about the Solar Sons and fear.

She scooped several deep breaths into her lungs.

He watched her breasts rise and fall with the effort. Forcing himself to look away, he focused on the freshly installed dead bolt. "Who has a key to your apartment?"

The bridge of Caroline's nose wrinkled in concentration. "Natalie, my mother." She shrugged as if she'd run out of names.

"How many keys do you personally have?"

"Three. No, two. One that I carry with me. One that I leave at the lab in the Quantum Building. I used to keep one at the research facility in Calumet, but I gave that key to Natalie."

Law nodded. He'd call Natalie and Caroline's mother to double-check on the location of their keys. That only left Caroline's two keys. "And the super has a master key, of course."

She jolted straighter in her chair. "You don't think Yashi let Hutch in, do you?"

"I don't know."

"When we first arrived, Mrs. Hansen said something about him spending a lot of time at my apartment. It sounded like she meant he'd been here recently. But why would he be spending time here when I was gone?"

"We'll check him out." Law made a mental note to ask Whitney to do just that. "Where is the key you carried with you?"

She thought for a moment, then gestured to the kitchen. "There are hooks on the wall just inside the door. It should be there, unless Hutch took it the night he kidnapped me." She raised her eyebrows in a hopeful question.

"That still wouldn't explain how he got in here that night."

"No." Her face fell.

Law stood and strode to the kitchen. Sure enough, a key dangled from one of the hooks. He returned to the dining room and held it out to Caroline. "Is this it?"

"Yes."

"When was the last time you saw the key you keep at the lab downtown?"

"I don't know."

He reached out a hand to assist her from her chair.

She put her hand in his, her fingers doeskin soft against his palm.

Longing shuddered up his arm and trembled through his body. He tore his gaze from her eyes, her lips, and focused on the door, trying not to notice how good her hand felt in his.

"Where are we going?"

"To your lab to find that key." And while they were there, he couldn't help but hope the lab where Caroline spent most of the waking hours of her life would help her rediscover her life. And her memory. Because if Hutch Greely was Gordon Doeller's murderer, as Law suspected, the sooner Caroline remembered the details of the murder, the sooner Greely would be behind bars and Caroline would be safe.

From the outside, Quantum Industries' headquarters looked like any other office building kneeling at the foot of the Sears Tower in Chicago's South Loop. Flowers dripped from window planters on the street level. Recently cleaned and restored by legions of workers and miles of scaffolding, the massive and slightly ornate concrete walls stretched to the sky in an imposing show of strength. And the glass doors opened into a marble entryway that gleamed wealth and success. But once Law and Caroline passed through the rotating door and into the building, the differences were obvious.

As a result of the recent terrorist assaults and the attempt to kidnap Natalie Van Buren, Quantum Industries was now tightened down like a fortress. Armed men in dark uniforms flanked the large metal detector at the entrance. Employees of Quantum wore ID badges around their necks, pausing to scan them into the computer at the reception desk before being allowed to enter the building, and then again at the elevators before being spirited to the upper floors.

Law and Caroline stopped at the reception desk. After enduring a long process of verifying who they were and signing in on the log, the front-desk receptionist gave Caroline an ID and Law a visitor's pass, and they were allowed inside.

After scanning their identification into one of the elevators, they stepped inside the car and Caroline hit the button for the floor that housed her lab. A low giggle touched with a note of desperation escaped her lips.

Law searched her face, concern welling inside him. "What's so funny?"

"I remember the floor on which I work. I remember my parents' phone number and birthdays. I even remember Sammy Sosa's batting average from last year. But who killed Gordon Doeller, how I feel about my family, anything important at all…" She held out her arms in a shrug, then dropped them to her sides.

"I know." Law ached to fold her into his arms, hold her close and tell her everything would be all right. That the answers she needed would be in her lab. That her life would return to normal. But he couldn't promise anything. He could only hope.

The elevator car stopped at the fifteenth floor and the door opened. Law followed Caroline down the hall and through an unmarked door.

The laboratory was impressive even to Law. Though he wasn't familiar with half the equipment that covered the granite-topped workbenches, he must be looking at the latest in technology. A far cry from Hutch's makeshift lab. The computer equipment alone was probably worth more than the entire Solar Sons compound.

"Caroline. It's nice to see you," a squeaky voice rang out.

Law followed the voice to a slightly built man. Sporting a white lab coat and a wispy, dark beard that was thinner than a seventeen-year-old's, the man raced across the lab with open arms.

"Jimmy." Caroline's voice held a genuine note of affection. She opened her arms and enfolded him in a hug.

Although Caroline's hug seemed platonic, Law wasn't so sure about Jimmy's. A totally inappropriate wave of jealousy lapped at the edges of Law's temper. He pushed the feeling away just in time to notice similar feelings emanating from the expression of a petite, pixielike woman on the other side of the lab.

Eyes hard and mouth pursed, the woman stared holes in Caroline, her dislike open and seething. She wore a white lab coat matching Jimmy's, but hers was buttoned to the neck. And her brunette hair was bound tight to her head in a twist.

The embrace ended between Caroline and Jimmy. Jimmy was the first to speak. "Sophie told me you joined the Solar Sons. Is that true?"

Law narrowed his eyes on Jimmy with renewed interest. "How do you know the Solar Sons?"

The little man shrugged. "They're that eco-cult, aren't they? The ones who use slogans about fighting for the earth? Sophie told me Caroline joined." He turned to look at the bitter-faced pixie.

She stared at Caroline. "I saw a story about them on the news. And Caroline was on the news, as well."

Of course. The tape Vincent had shown him. The one featuring a clearly brainwashed Caroline. Half the city saw that tape.

"Hi, Sophie." Caroline took a step toward her.

Sophie stood stock-still, her face wooden. Judging from the expression on her face, she'd rather spit on Caroline than hug her. "It's nice to see you, Caroline. Now, if you'll excuse me, I have to run some samples next door." Spinning on her heel, Sophie scampered from the lab, disappearing out a side door.

Seemingly unfazed by the brush-off, Caroline glanced around the lab as if admiring a work of art and took a deep breath, drawing in God-knew-what chemicals and fumes. "It's good to be back."

Law stepped beside her, watching her face for clues. "Memories?"

"Some. A lot, really. Mostly about my work. How I felt about it. How I still feel about it."

A perplexed look crossed Jimmy's face.

Law ignored him. He wasn't about to explain. He looked back to Caroline. "The key?"

"In my desk." She pointed to the section of the marble-topped counter that formed a desk. A desk chair sat in front of the area, and the same family photo of the Van Burens he'd seen in Caroline's bedroom perched on the surface. "The top drawer."

Law crossed to the desk and opened the drawer. It was filled with neatly stacked papers and a score of sharpened pencils. In the corner a key attached to a Chicago Cubs key ring peeked out from beneath some papers.

So the key hadn't gone missing. And with the kind of security bristling through the Quantum Building, he doubted Hutch had sneaked into the lab, used the key and returned it. But that didn't mean he wasn't going to check. There had to be some sort of explanation of how Hutch broke into Caroline's apartment, both the night of the kidnapping and in order to leave his calling card. And Law sure as hell wasn't leaving any stone unturned until he found out how. Using a piece of blank paper, he plucked the key from the drawer and folded it inside.

Jimmy watched the process, the perplexed look frozen on his face. Suddenly he seemed to jump out of his trance. "I almost forgot. You got a package marked Urgent today, Caroline."

Now it was Caroline's turn to look perplexed. "A package?"

"I'll get it." Jimmy spun and headed into one of the back rooms off the main lab.

Caroline's eyes found Law. Fear radiated from their blue depths.

"I'll look at it, Caroline. If it's another gift from Hutch, you don't need to see it."

She drew a deep breath and raised her chin. "No. I can handle it. I have to face Hutch. I can't spend my life hiding."

Though Law would prefer to open the package a mile away from Caroline, she was right. She did have to face Hutch and see how controlling and manipulative he was if she was going to fully shuck his influence.

She was off to a hell of a start. Despite her confusion over Doeller's death, despite her fear when she saw the card on her bed, she was recovering. With each hour that passed, she was returning to the woman she used to be. A woman who faced things head-on. A woman who wasn't about to allow him to protect her from reality. Law should be glad she'd insisted on facing the truth. It was another sign of her recovery.

But an uneasy pressure clamped down on his shoulders.

Jimmy returned to the lab, a standard brown shipping box in his hands. "Here it is. There's a knife over there to cut the tape." Releasing one side of the box, he pointed a finger to a penknife. The box bobbled in his grip. In his struggle to balance it, the side hit the marble counter.

Flames exploded from the box.

Chapter Seven

Caroline couldn't believe what she was seeing. Flame licked over the sleeves of Jimmy's lab coat and ignited his torso. His eyes grew wide. Flailing his arms, he beat at the fire.

"Get down and roll!" Law lunged for Jimmy and pushed him to the floor.

Caroline whirled for the extinguisher. The wire brackets that fastened it to the wall were empty. Panic surged through her. The fire extinguisher was always on the wall. What had happened to it?

Rolling Jimmy on the tile floor, Law beat at the flames with his hands.

Caroline scanned the lab, looking for something, anything that would retard the flame. The fire extinguisher sat on the edge of the workbench on the other side of Jimmy. She plunged forward. Her hand closed over the canister. Pointing the nozzle at Jimmy, she squeezed. White foam showered the flames, smothering them on contact. White spattered both Jimmy and Law. The sprinkler system overhead exploded, water spraying everywhere.

Through the smoke and water, Law hunched over

Jimmy, coughs wracking his frame. Jimmy groaned, but didn't move.

"Call 911," Law ordered.

Caroline darted for the phone and punched in the number. She gave the Cook County dispatcher the requested information just as Quantum security burst into the lab. They focused their weapons on Law. "What the hell's going on here?"

Law struggled to his feet. "Nothing. It was just an accident."

Caroline couldn't believe her ears. "An accident?" This fire was no accident. It was deliberate. Likely the package was designed to explode into flame as soon as she opened it. It was only an accident that Jimmy had bumped the box and set it off prematurely.

Law shot her a look, a silent message to keep quiet.

She glanced to the Quantum security guards and back to Law. Obviously Law was trying to hide the true nature of the fire from the guards. But why? A shiver scampered up her spine, but she kept her mouth closed. For now.

"This man is injured," Law barked. "I need some help here."

One of the security guards knelt next to Jimmy. The other headed for the phone on Caroline's desk.

"An ambulance is on its way," Caroline said. She raced to the spot next to the bracket where the fire extinguisher should have been and collected the first-aid kit, carrying it to Jimmy's side.

Jimmy looked up at her, his eyes round, his skin

blanched. Although he'd been burned, he didn't seem to be too badly hurt. But that didn't mean he wasn't in pain. A groan eked from his clenched lips.

"It's going to be all right, Jimmy." She tried to keep her voice even, but the scent of scorched flesh made her stomach buck and retch. Memories fluttered behind her eyes. Memories of the scent of gasoline, of truly burned flesh, of human screams. She could see the outline of a man striking a match. She could hear laughter bubble from his lips as he threw the match into the SUV. Her head throbbed.

A hand closed around her upper arm and pulled her up and away from the smell. Away from Gordon Doeller.

No. From Jimmy. Someone was pulling her from Jimmy, escorting her to a corner of the lab. Paramedics took her place over Jimmy.

"Are you all right?" Law's baritone splashed over her, refreshing as a slap of cool water. He leaned her against the solid workbench.

She searched his eyes. "I—I almost remembered. About Gordon Doeller."

"What did you remember?"

She tried to reach back into her mind, to grasp the memory. But she fell short. "It's no use. I saw a shadow. And heard his laugh."

"He laughed?" Law repeated, as if this was an important point.

"He laughed when he threw the match. I think." She looked past Law in time to see the paramedics preparing to load Jimmy on a stretcher. "How could this happen? One minute Jimmy is smiling, happy to see me, the next he's burning.''

Like Gordon Doeller had burned.

She was going to be sick. Or faint.

Law grasped her arm and lowered her into a chair. ''Put your head down.'' His hand clasping the back of her head, he folded her at the waist until her forehead rested between her knees. ''Now breathe.''

She did as he ordered, scooping mouthfuls of air into her lungs. Within seconds her mind began to clear and her stomach ceased its swirling.

When she was sure she'd be all right, she raised her head and met Law's concerned gaze as steadily as she could. ''It was Hutch, wasn't it?''

''I think so.'' He gestured to a small red mound of partially melted plastic peeking from the smoldering remains of the shipping box. ''A firebomb with plastic casing, designed to make it through metal screens.''

She looked at the mound of plastic. The fact that Hutch had used such a device and had addressed the package to her could only mean one thing. ''You were right. Hutch wants to kill me.''

Law nodded.

She glanced at the security guards. One of them helped the paramedics. The other switched on the ventilation system, and within seconds the lab was clear of smoke and the scent of burned flesh. ''Why did you tell the guards this was an accident?''

A muscle tightened along Law's jaw. ''Because I don't want anyone else at Quantum to know about this.''

"Why shouldn't they know about arson and attempted murder in the building where they work? They have the right to know."

"Because this isn't a simple case of arson and attempted murder."

"Then what is it?"

"It's terrorism, Caroline. And the fewer people that know about it at this point, the better."

A shock jolted through her. She remembered the explosion that had damaged Quantum's company office in Reykjavik, Iceland. The official story was that the explosion was caused by a gas leak. An explanation that had made Caroline uneasy.

But even with her suspicion about the cause of the explosion, the threat of terrorism had seemed remote to her. She'd worried about the possibility, but she'd never quite believed it would touch her life this intimately. "Are you saying Hutch is a terrorist?"

"He's been under investigation since before he kidnapped you. This is just one of many incidents."

"Incidents? What kind of incidents? Reykjavik?"

"No. We caught the men responsible for Reykjavik. At least most of them. We don't think Hutch was a part of that. The incidents we have reason to connect him with are closer to home. Fires at refineries owned by both Quantum and Petrol. A pipe bomb mailed to an executive at Petrol. Gordon Doeller's very symbolic murder."

"If Hutch did those things, why hasn't he been arrested?"

"The authorities can't arrest him without evidence. But this time he made a mistake."

"What kind of mistake?"

"In past strikes, he used accelerants and matches, pipe bombs, everyday devices that are available everywhere. But now he's gotten more advanced. And that's what is going to help us catch him. Incendiary devices like this one are harder to come by, and therefore easier to trace."

She tried to grasp his meaning, but the fear pounding through her head was too loud, her mind was too jumbled. She gave him a questioning look.

"This time Hutch left evidence. Evidence we can hopefully use to take him out of commission and keep him from hurting you ever again."

She looked back to the mound of melted plastic flecked with ash and white fire-extinguisher foam. Her mind latched on to Law's words. *Evidence we can use.* "We? Who's we?"

Law didn't answer.

"Law, who is *we?* You *promised* to tell me the *truth.*"

He plucked his cell phone from his jacket pocket and punched in a number. "In addition to my position at Petrol, I work for an agency called Chicago Confidential. I'm an undercover federal agent, Caroline."

CAROLINE FOLLOWED Law into an elevator in the Langston Building and watched him hit the button for the penthouse floor. She hadn't said two words to him after he'd confessed to her he was a federal agent. Not when he made the phone call to the agency. Not when Whitney and a technician named

Andy showed up to collect evidence. And not on the taxi ride from Quantum to the Langston Building in the north end of the Loop. Her own thoughts were so jumbled, she hadn't known what to say. Even now when she stared at the flashing numbers above the elevator door, her mind was void of words.

But it was filled with plenty of images. First the fire that had sent Jimmy to the hospital, then the realization that Hutch was trying to kill her. And to top it all off, Law threw in his admission that he worked for some government agency.

She felt him scan her face. "I wish I could have told you I was a federal agent before, Caroline."

She kept her gaze riveted to the flashing elevator numbers climbing closer and closer to the penthouse floor. A muscle worked in the smooth column of her throat. "Why didn't you?"

"Chicago Confidential is a secret, undercover agency. I shouldn't have told you even now about my cover."

"Why? Do you think I'll spread the news?" Her voice sounded bruised at the implication. Darn it, she *felt* bruised at the implication.

"I couldn't be sure you wouldn't lapse back into the thinking Hutch taught you."

"I wouldn't have."

"Do you know that? Honestly?"

She focused on the floor. She didn't know that. Her mind and emotions were in such a muddle, she didn't know anything for certain anymore.

"It's not that I didn't trust you, Caroline. But

you've been through a lot. Coercive persuasion techniques can take some time to overcome.''

Guilt niggled at the corners of her mind along with shame for succumbing to those techniques. She should have been able to resist. She should have been stronger. But she wasn't. "Aren't you worried that I'll tell someone now?''

"No.''

She looked up. "Why not? My mind isn't exactly clear yet.''

"It's clear enough.'' His green eyes drilled into her. "You don't have to feel ashamed.''

She opened her mouth, the denial poised on her tongue. A false denial, and she knew it. She drew in a deep breath. "I was weak. I gave up my freedom of will, of thought, of emotion. How am I supposed to feel?''

"Soldiers who have been trained to resist coercive persuasion have fallen victim to the types of techniques Greely used on you. And in a shorter time frame than you endured.''

"How is that supposed to make me feel better? I still gave up my very personality to follow Hutch. And I'm still not sure I won't fall back under his power.''

"You won't, Caroline. You're getting stronger every hour you're away from him. Besides, I'll be with you to make sure that doesn't happen.''

Images of Law with her, close to her, seeped through her mind. His arms around her. His hard chest pinning her to the wall. The heat of his lips descending on hers.

Impure images.

She was doing everything Hutch had warned her against. Being here with Law. Thinking about him that way. And now Hutch was trying to kill her for it. "What if Hutch tries again?"

"Don't worry about Hutch. He won't come near you. I'll make sure of it."

"How about the people around me? Who is going to keep them safe? He's already hurt Jimmy because of me." And he might even hurt Law. The thought cut into her like a sharp blade.

"Chicago Confidential is going to stop him, Caroline. That's why we're here."

The elevator chimed and the door slid open. Law ushered her from the car and into the wide hallway. She glanced around, taking in the rich green carpet and glass door etched with the logo of the floor's sole tenant. A computer consulting company. "Solutions, Inc.?"

"Chicago Confidential's mailing address. Step inside." He pulled open the door for her and followed her into the lobby.

A woman sat at a gleaming cherry reception desk. Although she was only maybe ten years older than Caroline's twenty-eight, her generous figure and dancing green eyes reminded Caroline of a doting nanny she and Natalie had as children. But this woman was much prettier. She didn't seem to notice Law and Caroline, her attention focused on something under the desk. "I said open. Don't you listen?"

A male voice answered from behind the desk. "I

know what the hell I'm doing, Kathy. Would you trust me for once?"

She shook her head, brown hair flecked with gold swinging against full cheeks. "I would trust you if you'd do what I ask."

"Even if I did every single thing you wanted, you wouldn't be satisfied. There's no satisfying a woman like you."

"You just have to give me what I need, Liam. And right now I need my drawers *open*."

Law cleared his throat.

The woman shot straight in her chair. "Oh my God. I mean, hello, Lawson. What can I help you with?" As a second thought, her attention moved to Caroline. A smile lifted her lips and dimpled one cheek. "Hello. I'm Kathy Renk. And this is Liam Wallace, the building's maintenance man."

Liam popped his male-model visage over the edge of the desk and gave them a quick nod of greeting before ducking back to his work.

Law settled a serious gaze on Kathy. "Is Vincent in?"

Kathy bobbed her head. "Everybody's inside. And Whitney called to say she and Andy are on their way back."

"Good. Could you get Caroline a cup of coffee or something while she waits?"

"I'll take good care of her."

Law gave Caroline a reassuring smile. "I'll be back before too long. If you need anything, just ask Kathy." He brushed her elbow with a hand in one last supportive gesture. Then he turned and headed down a hallway.

Caroline tried to ignore the warmth spreading through her at his simple touch. She couldn't think of Law right now. Of the way he'd helped her realize her devotion to Hutch was a lie, the way he'd taken care of her, the way he'd saved Jimmy's life. Her feelings for him were as jumbled as her thoughts. And the strong sexual pull that gripped her whenever he was around shook her to her toes.

She forced her eyes from the hall where he had disappeared and glanced around the lobby. The rich cherry furnishings and brocade chairs gave the room a classic air reminiscent of her family's home in Lake Forest. And like the Van Buren mansion, the scale and grandeur of the surroundings dwarfed her. As at the family home, she felt like nothing but a little sister, a burden, a person who had to be cared for.

She stared through the massive windows overlooking Lake Shore Drive and the Chicago harbor. She wouldn't just curl into the fetal position and let others take care of her. She hadn't given in to that temptation as a child, and she wouldn't give in to it now. She would face her problems. She would get her life back.

THE MEETING didn't last long. Vincent and Quint had already formulated a plan. They had only to wait for Andy and Whitney to arrive to map it out and begin implementation. Before an hour had passed, they had all worked out the details, and Law was on his way back to Caroline.

Reaching the lobby, he stopped and watched her. She looked so small and vulnerable in the spacious and elegant lobby. She'd grown up in surroundings like this. The best furnishings, a view of the lake, but somehow she didn't fit the elegance. She belonged much more to her little apartment in Lincoln Park or her laboratory in Quantum.

He drew a deep breath. He was letting his mind wander. Letting his imagination take him where he wished it could go. It wasn't his place to decide where she belonged. His job was only to keep her safe and get on with the mission at hand—the mission to put Hutch Greely and the Solar Sons out of the terrorism business.

She turned in his direction. A smile fluttered over her lips for a moment, then died. Her forehead creased with obvious concern.

Man, he must be easy to read.

She pushed herself up from the chair. "What's going to happen? What did you decide?"

He closed the distance between them in a few strides. "Come with me." He probably didn't have to worry about Kathy hearing what he had to say, but he had the feeling Caroline wasn't going to like this plan. Not one little bit. And he'd rather keep the inevitable argument private.

He touched her elbow with his fingers, ushering her down the hallway and into an office filled with computer accessories and a wide window overlooking the lake.

Caroline took in the surroundings. "So there really is a computer business here?"

"Yes. Solutions, Inc. does computer and telecommunications work while not on assignment. They're very good and very high priced, but worth every penny.

She nodded as if satisfied and focused on the window and the undulating waves outside. "What are you going to do? About Hutch, I mean."

Law folded himself into a chair and gestured for Caroline to sit, as well. Once she had, he looked her straight in the eye. Although she was breaking away from Hutch's influence every hour she'd been away from the compound, he still wasn't sure what her reaction would be to their plan. But he was certain she wouldn't like her part in it. Not one bit. It was important he make her accept it if he was to keep her safe. And as far as he was concerned, that was what it was all about. Keeping Caroline safe. "We're going to infiltrate the Solar Sons."

No reaction from Caroline. So far, so good.

"Andy is going in undercover."

"Andy?" Her eyes seemed to brighten at the name. "The guy collecting evidence at the lab?"

"He's the one. We need him to match the incendiary device at the lab with any that might be in the Solar Sons' arsenal. He's the expert."

She gave him a nod of confidence.

Law could tell she'd liked Andy when she'd met him at the lab. Not surprising. And judging from his eager smile and nonstop chatter, Andy liked her, as well. They were of like scientific minds. A regular admiration society. "He's going to the earth rally tomorrow in Springfield. If everything goes as planned, he'll get recruited into the cult. We'll give him a few days before we go in.''

A little crease dug between her eyebrows. ''What do you mean by going in? Most of the cult members aren't militaristic, you know. The men Hutch calls his 'Solar Guard' are the only ones who are armed.''

''We aren't going in with guns blazing, if that's what you're afraid of. Vincent will go in first, over the fence. He and Andy will take out the front guard and separate the unarmed cult members from Hutch and his guards. Quint and I will take care of Hutch and his men.''

''Just you and Quint? There are six men in Hutch's Solar Guard. And they have machine guns and—''

''We're going in at night. We're counting on the element of surprise to keep this from turning into a battle. If there's any sign that they've caught on to us, we abort the plan.''

''Why don't you just get more men?''

''We're trying to keep this as low-key as possible. We don't want another mistake like some agencies have made in past years.'' He gave her what he hoped was a reassuring smile. The thought that she was worried about him felt better than it should. ''Don't worry. Vincent has run this kind of operation before. He knows what he's doing.''

''I think I can tell you what is in most buildings in the compound, and where people sleep.''

''That would be helpful.''

''So what else can I do to help?''

The tendons in Law's shoulders tightened. ''Just

give us the locations. That will be great. We'll take it from there.''

She narrowed her eyes, as if zeroing in on what he wasn't saying. ''And where will I be during this operation?''

He might as well get it out of the way. ''I'm taking you to your parents' house tonight.''

''No.''

''You'll be safe there. Your father has hired extra security. He says the house is like a fortress. Hutch will never reach you there.''

''I'm not worried about Hutch. I'm not staying at my parents' house. I'm not ready to face them. Not yet.''

''I know it will be hard sorting through all Hutch told you.''

''It's more than that. I can't just sit around and have people take care of me. Especially my family. I can't see them until I know who I am again. Until I know what's true and what isn't.''

Law stood and paced to the window. Staring out at the white sails bobbing on the lake, he tried to come up with ways to convince her. His mind was blank.

He heard her stand and felt her walk up behind him. ''Take me with you. I can help.''

He turned to face her. ''Absolutely not. I'm trying to protect you, not usher you into Greely's arms.''

''Putting Hutch in jail is the only thing that will protect me and allow me to return to my life.''

''And we'll do that. Leave it to Chicago Confidential.''

"I have to face Hutch. I can't run away. Let me help."

"No. If you don't go to Lake Forest, I'll hire security to protect you."

She crossed her arms over her chest. "I won't help you map the compound unless you'll agree to take me along."

Damn. She had him over a barrel this time. Knowing the locations of Hutch's soldiers and armory might make the difference between a successful mission and utter failure. But the price she demanded was too high. "I'm not taking you with me into the compound, Caroline. You do whatever you have to."

Her mouth tensed with obvious frustration.

For a moment he felt sorry for her. He could imagine how it felt to be so powerless. So lost. The way he'd felt after resigning from the state's attorney's office. His life's work gone, he'd had no idea who he was anymore. But of course, Caroline's loss was more substantial than that. She'd lost her entire sense of self.

But risking her life by marching into the Solar Sons compound was not the way to find herself.

"What if I stay on the fringes? Away from the compound?"

He exhaled a stream of air through tight lips. He obviously wasn't going to be able to talk her into staying at her parents' house. And having her closer to him did make him feel inexplicably better. Whitney would be in the mobile unit, in constant radio contact with Chicago Confidential agents. Caroline could stay with her. Surely she'd be safe there.

He looked at Caroline. He sure as hell hoped he wasn't making a mistake. He couldn't afford any kind of mistake. Not with Caroline's life on the line. "I'll see what I can do."

Chapter Eight

Three days later, Caroline watched Law and Quint load the van with an array of weapons and bullet-proof vests. A shiver inched up her spine and wrapped around her chest. She'd always hated guns. She'd grown up in a house void of any kind of weapon but the kitchen butcher knife. She'd never even seen a gun in real life until Natalie had taken up target practice on her self-defense kick. But now, watching Law carry big guns and small to the van parked in the private bay of the parking garage under the Langston Building, she just hoped they had enough firepower to subdue Hutch and his Solar Guard.

Pressure closed around her chest and squeezed. She was going to the compound. She was going to see this through, but somehow that didn't make her feel better. It wasn't only her fear of Hutch that nagged at her. It was something more. Something she didn't want to examine too closely.

"Looks like we're almost ready." Law secured the weapons in the back of the van and jumped down

to join her. He studied her with concerned eyes.
"How are you holding up?"

She avoided his gaze. "Fine. I'm ready."

He lifted an eyebrow, as if skeptical of her claim.
"You could stay here, you know."

"This is my battle, Law."

"Maybe. But you don't have to put yourself
within range of his gun in order to face him."

She'd never seen Hutch himself hold a gun. He'd
always left that to the earth brothers surrounding
him. His Solar Guard. But that didn't mean she
couldn't imagine how he'd look with a deadly
weapon in his hand. He'd described more than once
and in intricate detail how he planned to press the
muzzle of a gun between her eyes and pump a bullet
into her brain. "I won't be within the range of his
gun. Whitney said we'd be far from the action, if
there is any. It's you that's putting yourself in front
of Hutch's guns." Fear chilled her at the thought of
Law in harm's way. He'd risked his life to rescue
her from the cult and again to beat out the fire that
engulfed Jimmy. She couldn't bear the thought of
him getting hurt trying to protect her yet again.

"It's my job."

"That's another question eating at me, another
part of this that doesn't make sense."

"Why I'm part of Chicago Confidential?"

"Yes. You're a lawyer. You have a career. How
can you moonlight as a federal agent? Isn't that a
full-time career as well?"

"Chicago Confidential is different. It's undercover, *confidential*. Our careers act as our covers."

"I still don't understand. Being a federal agent isn't the same as having a little hobby on the side. You risk your life."

He shrugged, but the glower in his eyes was far darker than the casual gesture suggested. "Let's just say it's my penance."

"Penance? What was your sin?"

His lips twisted. "I sold my soul. And Chicago Confidential is my chance to buy it back."

"By paying for it with your life?"

He shook his head and hefted a box of ammunition into the van. "It's flattering that you're worried about me, Caroline. But you don't have to be. I'll come out of this mission just fine. And I'll get Greely. You can bet on it."

She sure hoped so. Because she didn't know what she would do if Law was hurt.

Or worse.

LAW GLANCED OVER his shoulder at the dark outline of the van, nearly hidden in the burgeoning waves of corn. Caroline and Whitney were a good mile from the Solar Sons compound, but it wasn't far enough away for him. He'd give anything to have her in Lake Forest, hunkered down in an impenetrable fortress with armed guards watching over her.

He drew a deep breath of humid country air and looked up at the millions of stars, like bullet holes in a dark canopy. The worry in Caroline's eyes ate at him. Although she made a feeble attempt at extending her concern to the other agents, he knew she was worried about *him*.

And that made *him* worried. Damn worried.

Caroline was the most passionate, giving woman he'd ever met. Five years ago, he hadn't been right for her, and time hadn't changed the situation. If anything, he was more jaded, more cynical, and less suitable for her now.

He'd told her Chicago Confidential was his penance, and he'd meant it. When Vincent had recruited him, he'd given Law the chance to make up for selling out to Petrol, given him the chance to erase all the selfish decisions he'd made. And one of those decisions was taking advantage of Caroline five years ago and not contacting her after.

And now Chicago Confidential was giving him the chance to make up for that sin, as well. The chance to ensure Caroline's safety and restore her life. And he'd sure as hell better come through this time.

''Is everyone in place?'' Whitney's soft East Coast accent drifted over the radio.

Each agent checked in. Vincent deep in the cornfield behind the compound. Law and Quint ready to enter the front gate. Andy was the cult's new recruit and didn't have a radio. They couldn't take the chance Hutch would order him frisked the way he'd done to Law before allowing him inside the cult's gates.

Law studied the outline of the farmhouse, a hulking shadow in the night. According to Caroline, Hutch and his Solar Guard lived in the farmhouse along with the armory. The rest of the members didn't have access to weapons. The setup made their mission easier than he could have hoped. With the

Solar Guard in one place, Quint and he shouldn't have too much trouble subduing them. Not with a little luck and surprise on their side.

"All right," Whitney called in a tight voice. "Move."

Law sprang to his feet. Half crouching, he ran through the corn toward the front gate, Quint behind him. When they reached the gate, both crouched low to the ground.

Law peered through the cornstalks at the secured gate. The loops of razor wire topping the gate and fence glinted in the feeble light from the quarter moon. Everything looked as it had before—the night Law rescued Caroline out of the Solar Sons' clutches. Everything except—

"Where the hell is the guard?"

Corn rustled as Quint crawled alongside him. "Could Andy have already taken him out?"

An uneasy cramp descended on Law's shoulders. "Maybe." He wanted that to be the case. But they couldn't bet on it. They had to be ready for anything.

"Maybe guard boy is checking out the back fence where Vincent went over."

Law nodded. That was a better possibility. Still... "Keep your eye out. He could know we're here."

Quint's head bobbed. He raised his pistol and focused on the gate, narrowing his eyes like a sheriff straight out of the Old West. "We don't need any surprises, that's for damn sure."

Law crawled close to the gate. He reached into the belt of tools and extra rounds circling his waist and pulled out a pair of heavy-duty wire cutters. He set to work snipping the thick wire. Finally the section of fence he was working on broke free, leaving a hole just big enough to squeeze through. He ducked through the hole and emerged on the other side. He raised his weapon, covering as Quint followed.

"Couldn't you have made this damn mouse hole a little bigger? Not everyone is as small as you."

Law smirked in Quint's direction. At five-eleven, Law wasn't exactly small. But Quint measured six feet three inches before he added the cowboy boots. And just like a Texan, he couldn't resist pointing out the difference in height. "Next time I'll cut the whole damn section out for you. Now suck it up and get inside before someone spots you."

Grinning, Quint quickly crawled through the fence and hunkered down next to Law in the shadow of the guardhouse.

No sound came from the compound. So far, so good. Now they were inside, they had to be precise about each step. One slip and the whole operation could come crashing down around their ears.

Crouching, they ran toward the farmhouse. Hopefully Vincent was inside, safe and sound. Between him and Andy, the majority of the cult members would be contained where they wouldn't be hurt. Quint and Law would take care of Greely and his armed guard.

Reaching the house, they crouched behind a row of lilac bushes framing one side of the house. Law gestured to the back of the house. "You take the front door, I'll take the back."

Quint smiled, his sun-bronzed skin crinkling at the

corners of his eyes. "I reckon I'll skip ringing the bell."

"You actually seem to be enjoying this, cowboy."

"You're not?" Quint focused those twinkling blue eyes in Law's direction. "I forgot, you're a lawyer. You probably prefer a stuffy courtroom as your battlefield."

Law couldn't argue with him. No matter what he'd said to Caroline about penance, he did prefer the tense air of the courtroom right before opening statements to running around playing commando. But he had to admit, it was growing on him. At least a little. "I'll like it just fine once we have Greely in handcuffs."

"Then let's roll." Hunching his big body forward, Quint ran closer to the house's front door.

Law circled the bushes, his pulse pounding in his ears. He crossed a small patio and sidled up to the back door. If the door was locked, he'd have to break in, creating noise that would ruin the element of surprise. He grasped the steel doorknob. The mechanism turned smoothly. Unlocked. Just as Caroline's door had been unlocked the night he'd rescued her. He pushed the door open and slipped inside.

The house was dark, and he had to hesitate for a moment to let his eyes adjust. He gripped his weapon in his hands, ready for any movement, any sound in the silent house.

Nothing came.

He moved through the house, clearing one room before advancing into another. Each room was filled with battered furniture. A harvest-gold shag carpet straight out of the early seventies covered the floor. Although the rooms were certainly worn, they seemed clean.

And empty.

Law met Quint at the staircase in the center of the house. "They must all be upstairs."

"Or not home."

Law's gut tightened. What if Hutch had seen through Andy's cover story? What if his men were waiting among the cottages right now? Vincent wouldn't stand a chance against a half-dozen armed-and-ready men. And who knew what Hutch would do to Andy?

Law forced the ugly images from his mind and focused on the staircase. Chances were the men were all upstairs asleep. And he and Quint had to stick to their plan until they discovered differently.

Law gave Quint a sharp nod and started up the stairs. He could hear Quint's breathing behind him, but nothing else. No sound from upstairs or down.

Reaching the top of the staircase, Law and Quint took turns covering and advancing through the hall. They swept through bedroom after bedroom. They were all empty.

"Damn. I hope Vincent was ready for them." Quint muttered as if reading Law's mind.

Law spoke into the microphone attached to his Kevlar vest. "Whitney? Have you heard from Vincent? What's happened to Vincent?"

"He hasn't checked in yet. Vincent? Come in, Vincent."

No answer.

Either Vincent's radio wasn't working, or Law's fears weren't as unfounded as he had hoped. "The house is clear, Whitney. We're heading for the cottages to find Vincent and Andy."

"All right." Even over the airwaves, her voice held an obvious note of worry for her husband.

Completing his sweep of the last bedroom on the upper level, Law paused near the plush queen-size bed in the middle of the room. Probably Hutch's room. He looked up at the mirror over the bed. Something red caught his eye. Red and plastic and deadly.

Law's pulse picked up its pace. Quint, too, was looking at the spot of red plastic with round eyes. He caught Quint's attention from across the room. "Let's get the hell out of here."

"Damn straight."

They sprinted from the room and ran down the narrow hall to the stairs. Law heard the explosion over the thunk of Quint's boots on the steps. Explosions echoed through the house, one after another. Fire consumed battered furniture. Smoke choked oxygen from the air.

Law burst out the house's side door, half expecting to be greeted with a hail of gunfire. Instead, he faced a compound as deserted as a ghost town. Quint made it out behind him, his weapon clutched ready in his hand. Law scanned the compound for any sign of Vincent or Andy. In the middle of the compound, a single cottage burned as furiously as the house. Caroline's cottage.

Smoke clogged thick in the back of Law's throat.

He turned to Quint. "Somehow Hutch knew our plans. He's destroying evidence."

"Maybe. But I don't like the timing of that fire-bomb. It couldn't be a coincidence that it went off while we were inside."

Quint was right. The ache in Law's shoulders intensified. He raked the shadows of the cottages with his gaze. Were some of the Solar Sons out there, watching, their fingers poised over detonators that would send the entire compound up in flames?

He leveled a hard gaze on Quint. "We have to find Vincent and Andy. I'm not leaving without them."

"I'm with you."

They jogged off in the direction of the cottages. The soft, tilled earth of vegetable gardens sucked at Law's boots. Reaching the closest cottage, Quint assumed a position of cover as Law pushed open the door. He flattened himself against the wall and covered Quint as the tall cowboy entered the room. The cottage was similar to Caroline's cottage, an austere single room, but this one was furnished with a bed. The sheets were rumpled, as if someone had left in a hurry in the middle of the night. He crossed the room and checked the closet. Empty.

They checked two more cottages, each empty, each looking as though they were evacuated in a hurry. They moved to the fourth cottage and burst inside. It was like the others, with one important difference. A padlock fastened the metal hasps on the flimsy closet doors.

"Cover me while I get these doors open."

Quint did as he asked, keeping his eye and his gun focused on the door.

With the tools in his belt, it took Law even less time to dismantle the hinges than it had when he'd found Caroline. He lifted the door off the hinges and set it against the wall. Andy lay at the bottom of the closet. Wrists and ankles bound, he turned his bruised face toward them and squinted to focus.

"It's Law, Andy."

He smiled as much as a split lip would allow. "I never thought you guys would look so good."

Law grabbed his arm and lifted him from the closet floor. "You must be in worse shape than I thought."

"You look like hell, Andy." Quint interjected from the doorway.

Another smile struggled to stretch over Andy's lips. "I guess undercover work isn't as cool as I thought."

Grasping a knife from his belt, Law cut the ropes. Andy's wrists were red with rope burn. Law helped Andy to his feet. The genius sagged against him, unable to stand on his own. Andy was hurt. And badly.

Law could only hope internal bleeding wasn't the cause of his weakness. "We'll talk about it after we get the hell out of here. Who knows how many more incendiary devices Greely planted around this place."

Quint draped one of Andy's arms around his shoulders and started for the door. Once outside, he froze in his tracks. Law stopped behind him.

Gravel crunched under boots. Someone was approaching from around the side of the cottage.

All three flattened against the cottage wall, Law and Quint holding their weapons at the ready.

Vincent burst around the corner, gun in the lead. Spotting them, he lowered his weapon. "You found him." He seemed to visibly relax, if Vincent ever really relaxed.

"What the hell happened? Where's your radio?"

"It snagged on the fence as I was going over. Let's get out of here before this whole place goes up in flames."

Wordlessly agreeing, they started for the front gate.

"Wait," Andy mumbled.

Vincent turned a black stare on him. "What is it?"

"The incendiary device. I smuggled one into my cabin. It's under the mattress." He tried to break out of Quint's grip as if intending to go back for it himself.

Law held up a hand in front of him. "I'll get it. You're in no shape." He turned to Vincent. "He needs to get back to the mobile unit. I'm afraid he might have some internal bleeding."

Vincent nodded. "We'll take him. Get the device and meet us back there."

Law jogged back in the direction of the cottage where they'd found Andy. The farmhouse was burning furiously now, belching smoke into the night sky. Law tried to keep his breathing shallow. He finally reached the cottage. The door stood as wide as a screaming mouth. He readied his weapon and pushed inside. The hulking shape of the bed loomed in the shadowed darkness. He crossed the room.

A floorboard creaked behind him. Before he could turn around, a heavy bat cracked against his skull.

He plunged into blackness.

Chapter Nine

Law's lungs burned. Heat licked at his face, his hands. His cheek rested against rough wood. Where was he? In hell?

He forced his eyes open and struggled to see through the thick air. His eyes refused to focus. His head spun.

The cottage. He'd come back to the cottage. He'd been attacked. The side of his head throbbed. He raised his hand to his temple. Something warm and sticky coated his fingers. Blood.

And the crackling of fire raged around him.

Damn. He had to get out of here. If he didn't, he was dead.

He forced himself to sit upright. His stomach bucked. Choking back nausea, he climbed to his knees. The bed. He'd come back to the cottage to retrieve the incendiary device under the mattress. He crawled on his hands and knees toward the hulking shape he hoped was the bed. Sure enough, his fingers found rumpled sheets. He groped for the bottom edge of the mattress. His fingers slipped underneath and hit something hard and plastic. He grabbed it and pulled.

The smoke was so thick, he couldn't see. Cradling the device in his hand, he crawled in the direction he remembered being the door. The wood panel was closed. He rammed his shoulder into it with all his strength. The flimsy wood cracked. The door gave, and he tumbled out into the fresh air.

Behind him, the fire whooshed, consuming the fresh dose of oxygen and reaching for more.

"SOMETHING MUST HAVE happened to him." Panic spiked Caroline's blood. She struggled to push past Quint's large frame. Law should be here by now. Something must have gone wrong. Something—

Quint grasped her arm. "And you think you're going to storm in there and save him? You're more like your sister than I'd realized."

"I can't just leave him in there. I have to—"

"You have to sit down and wait." Vincent loomed over her, his dark eyes commanding. He fitted a new tiny radio transmitter into his ear. "Quint and I will go back in for him."

Caroline clutched her hands together until her fingers ached from the pressure. When she'd first seen flame bursting from the compound, it had taken every once of self-control in her to prevent herself from dissolving into screams. Thankfully, the men had checked in with Whitney after the fire had started. But now… Now Law was out there alone. And he wasn't answering his radio.

Caroline's stomach rolled. She'd seen the second surge of fire. Fire that could have—

No. She couldn't think that way. Law had to be all right. He'd promised. He couldn't let her down now.

"Lawson, are you there?" Whitney barked over the radio for the hundredth time. Come in, Lawson."

Static answered her.

Whitney's eyes focused on Caroline's face. "Vincent and Quint will find him. Don't worry."

Don't worry. Caroline bit her lip. Fear screamed in her mind. *Don't worry.* She chanted the words like a mantra.

"You care about him, don't you?" Whitney said. Her gray gaze rested briefly on Caroline, before turning back to the silhouettes of cornstalks.

Caroline drew in a sharp breath. She did. In the past week he'd saved her from the Solar Sons, he'd helped her break through Hutch's lies, and he'd protected her. Of course she cared about him.

"I thought so," Whitney said without waiting for a response. "It's in the way you look at him. I'd recognize that look anywhere. It's the way I looked at Vincent shortly after we met."

Caroline brushed her hair back from her cheek. A shiver of recognition spread over her skin. Was Whitney right? Did she look at Law a certain way? Did she feel more than simple gratitude for his help?

Memories niggled at the back of her mind. Memories of Law's touch, the flavor of his kiss, the power of his desire for her. And her desire for him.

And the pain when he'd never called.

A weight settled in the pit of Caroline's stomach. She'd lost Law before. She couldn't lose him now. No matter how she felt or didn't feel. No matter how wrong her feelings were. Law had to be all right.

Silence stretched over the radio airwaves. Silence that chilled Caroline to the bone.

Finally a voice broke through. Vincent's voice. "We've reached the cottage where we left him. The place is almost burned to the ground. No sign of Lawson."

Caroline buried her face in her hands. Pain wracked her body, but she didn't cry. The tears wouldn't come. It was as if they had disappeared into the hole of deadness deep inside her.

"Damn." The curse sounded strange coming from Whitney's well-bred lips.

Caroline raised her eyes. Whitney pulled a pistol from her handbag and slid the safety off. Face ashen, she stared out into the cornfield.

Caroline followed her gaze. The corn in front of the van rustled, as if someone was creeping through the stalks.

Whitney gripped her arm, her manicured nails digging into Caroline's flesh. "Keep your head down." Clutching her gun in one hand, Whitney rolled down the window of the van and opened the door. Thrusting the gun through the open window in both hands, she assumed a shooting stance, using the door as a shield. "Federal agent. Stop immediately and put your hands on top of your head."

Caroline squinted into the darkness. The silhouette

of a man stopped dead in the corn. Slowly, he placed one hand on top of his head.

The movement struck a chord inside her. The silhouette was so familiar, so— ''Law.'' Caroline threw open the van's door and dived into the corn. She ran toward him on wobbly legs.

She could see him better as she drew close. Blood caked his hair and trickled down the side of his face. He'd been hurt. Oh God, Law had been hurt.

But he was alive.

He looked at her with dark eyes and half stumbled, half limped toward her, something red clutched in one hand.

She caught him in her arms. She strained upward toward him. Her lips found his face, his hair, his lips. The flavor of dust and smoke and blood filled her senses. But under it all was Law. He was safe.

His arms slipped around her and he leaned heavily against her. ''I told you I'd make it back.''

THE DEAD BOLT of Chicago Confidential's safe house's front door turned.

Sitting on the living-room couch, Caroline tensed. Quint said he'd be out in front, keeping watch over the house just in case Hutch had somehow discovered where she was the same way he'd discovered Chicago Confidential's plan to arrest him and his militant followers. It was probably Quint himself opening the door. She probably had no reason to worry. But dread inched up her spine anyway.

She stood, poised to do something. Fight or flight, she didn't know.

The door swung wide. Law stepped into the safe house, leaning against the door as if he needed help staying on his feet.

Relief shot through Caroline, chased by surprise. "What are you doing here? You were supposed to stay in the hospital another night for observation, weren't you?"

Law lifted a hand to touch his bandaged head, as if reminding himself of his injury. "I don't need to be observed any longer. I said I'd protect you, so here I am."

Caroline frowned. One of the other agents could protect her. Quint had been on the job since they'd returned last night. He'd only gone outside for a breath of air. "How did you get the doctor to release you?"

"He didn't exactly." Law's lips twisted in a sardonic smile. He plodded up the half flight of stairs to the level where Caroline stood, his hand on the rail for support. "I said I'd protect you, and I meant it."

"I appreciate the sentiment, but you don't look like you're in shape to protect anything."

"I can handle it."

There was obviously no way to win this argument. "All right. You can handle protecting me. I believe you. Now go back to the hospital where you belong. Quint and I were doing just fine."

"Quint is on his way to Wisconsin."

"Wisconsin? Why Wisconsin?"

"We have reason to believe Hutch is heading up that way. He might be going to Canada." His lips twisted into a bitter line. "I'm obviously in no shape to go after him."

Hutch was gone. She was safe. And not only that, she and Law were once again alone.

Her pulse quickened. She thought of kissing him in the cornfield. If she closed her eyes, she could still feel the warmth of his lips against hers, still smell the scent of his skin. And somewhere deep inside, she yearned for more. "Whitney said you have a concussion. You shouldn't be walking around. If I can't convince you to go back to the hospital, let me at least get you into bed."

His head snapped around, and his eyes met hers. There was no mistaking the path his thoughts were taking.

The same place her thoughts had wanted to roam just seconds before. She felt the heat rise up her neck. Her nerves jittered, as if she'd downed two pots of coffee. "I mean, why don't you lie down? I'll help you."

"All right." The heat didn't fade from his eyes. "I'll lie on the couch. I want to be able to keep an eye on the door."

She slipped an arm around his rib cage in order to help him across the room. But he didn't lean on her for balance. He moved quite steadily, as if he needed her closeness more than her help.

The heat of his body seeped into her. The jittering in her blood picked up its pace until her whole body felt as if it was jumping out of her control. She nearly sighed with relief when she lowered him to the couch and perched on the edge of the coffee table, an arm's length away.

He arranged the pillows behind his head so he was half sitting facing the door. He drew his pistol from his shoulder holster and set it in his lap. His movements were swift and sure, though pain was evident in the tightness of his mouth and the way his eyes narrowed.

"This is ridiculous. You're in no shape to stand guard. What are you going to do if Hutch comes through that door?"

"Shoot him."

He was impossible. No matter how much he was hurting, no matter what she said, he wasn't moving from his post. But that didn't mean she'd leave him to his guard duty. Too much had happened last night. Too much hadn't been explained. And she wanted some answers. If Law was feeling well enough to stand guard, he was well enough to give her some answers.

"How could Hutch have known you were coming to the compound last night?"

"Damn good question."

"And the answer?"

"I don't know. Andy didn't know he'd been found out until they were tying him up and stuffing him in the closet."

"If Andy didn't give the operation away, then who?" She thought of the way Hutch had gained access to her apartment seemingly at his whim. The way he'd gotten the package through Quantum security, as if he'd known just how to fool Jimmy and bypass security. "Hutch seems to know my life better than I do."

"What do you mean?"

"He can get into my apartment and penetrate the security in my lab without anyone being the wiser. And now he figures out your plans almost before I know you're a federal agent."

"Someone is feeding him information. It's the only explanation."

Law's words slithered down Caroline's spine. He was right. It was the only explanation. Hutch wasn't all knowing and invincible. No matter what he'd made her believe when she was locked in that tiny closet hanging on his every word. "Who would feed him that kind of information?"

"Another good question." Law held his hand to his head for a moment, as if seized by pain.

"Maybe we shouldn't talk right now. Maybe you should rest." She started to rise from the edge of the table.

He grasped her wrist, holding her fast. His eyes bore into her. "Stay. It will help to talk about the possibilities."

She didn't know if it would help her or him, but it didn't matter. She lowered herself back onto the edge of the table. "Whoever it was had to have access to my apartment key."

"And have knowledge about your life."

"My neighbor, Mrs. Hansen."

He mulled this over for a moment. "She should have heard something the night of your kidnapping."

"And come to think of it, I gave her my key once

to water my plants when I was away on business and my family was gone and couldn't take care of it. I figured it would be better to have Mrs. Hansen in the apartment than a complete stranger."

"So she had access to your key, and she knows your lifestyle. But she wouldn't have any way of knowing what we were planning last night."

"No." She thought for a moment. "How about Sophie, my lab assistant?"

Law nodded, then winced slightly with pain. "She did have access to the key in your desk. And she certainly doesn't seem to like you much."

Caroline blew out an exasperated breath. "I think she has a crush on Jimmy and sees me as some sort of rival. It's ridiculous. Anyone can see that she and Jimmy would be perfect together."

"She might have a legitimate complaint."

"What?" Caroline couldn't believe her ears. Did Law believe she and Jimmy— Impossible. "Jimmy and I are friends and co-workers. Nothing more."

"He definitely has a crush on you."

"Why on earth would he have a crush on me?"

"Why wouldn't he? You're an incredible woman. Bright, sexy, passionate about life." Law's eyes grew darker, more intense. "An incredible woman."

She felt as if he was seeing all of her—her thoughts, her feelings, her secret dreams—open and exposed. But she couldn't look away. She raised her fingers to her lips, touching the spot his lips had touched only yesterday. The spot she wanted them to touch again.

Law broke eye contact first. He cleared his throat,

as if reaching for words he couldn't locate. Finally he looked back into her eyes, his face composed. "And has Sophie been to your apartment?"

Caroline tried to calm her mind. Her nerves were humming, her heart beating loud enough for Law to hear. "Yes. She and Jimmy and I have gone to Cubs' games together. My apartment isn't far from Wrigley, so it's been our meeting spot."

He nodded as if adding this tidbit to his mental file.

"And then there's Yashi, the superintendent of my building. He has a key, of course. He could let anyone into my apartment at any time. But none of these people knew about Chicago Confidential's plan to infiltrate the Solar Sons compound. And none of them would know you're a federal agent. Even I didn't know when we were at my apartment. And Sophie had thankfully left the lab before Jimmy was burned, so she couldn't have overheard you tell me." Caroline shuddered at the memory of the fire. She was grateful Sophie hadn't been there and hadn't seen the burns Jimmy suffered. The poor girl would never have been able to handle it.

"There's another possibility."

"What's that?"

"Maybe the leak isn't coming from someone in your life."

"Then who? The only other people who know about all this are the other Chicago Confidential agents."

His silence spoke volumes.

"You think it's another agent?"

He sighed. "Not really. I can't see any of them betraying the mission. Not for anything. But until I figure out who is informing Greely of our every move, I'm not ready to trust anyone."

She swallowed into a dry throat. She knew the fear of trusting, the fear of being lied to, the fear of betrayal that he spoke of. She still couldn't bring herself to talk to her family, to sort through what was real and what wasn't. And Hutch— She was still trying to fight through the lies he'd told her.

She looked back into Law's eyes. She may not know who to trust in the outside world. But right now, right here, she knew she could trust Law Davies with her life. She just hoped she could also trust him with her heart. Because it was getting more and more difficult to deny that her heart was very much involved.

Chapter Ten

Law hung up the phone. It had been so long since he'd gotten some good news, he hardly knew how to react. Four days had passed since Chicago Confidential agents had gone in to close down the Solar Sons eco-cult, only to find a deserted compound rigged to burn and someone waiting to knock him over the head. His head had improved in the past days, both the gash at his hairline and the concussion that went with it. But that was the only thing that had improved with time.

After Caroline's grateful kisses the night of the failed mission, he was having a hell of a time being cooped up with her without touching her. If he had to spend another four days listening to Caroline's breathing and soft moans as she slept in the bedroom next to his, or picture the soap sluicing over her curves as she took her morning shower, he would go mad.

He had to do something, anything to speed up the search for Hutch. They were reasonably certain the incendiary device he'd recovered at the compound matched the one Hutch had sent to Caroline's lab.

As soon as Andy was released from the hospital and could study the devices in depth, they would be sure. But that didn't mean they hadn't been tracking Hutch. And now they may have found him. And in light of the news he'd just heard, it should be safe to leave the town house and track down some of the other questions in this case. And what better day to start than today?

"Have they found Hutch?" Caroline's voice rose over the soft padding of her footsteps on plush carpet. Step by step, her bare legs came into view on the stairs leading to the kitchen above.

Law stifled a groan. Why couldn't it be the dead of winter? At least then she could dress in sweatpants and a baggy shirt. Shorts and little T-shirts were killing him. He turned away, forcing himself to peer between the window-blind slats and not at those delicious legs. "Whitney dug up a large land purchase in northern Wisconsin, near Lake Superior. There have also been sightings of some cult members in the area. It seems the Solar Sons have put down roots again."

He heard her reach the bottom of the stairs and walk across the carpet toward him. She stopped behind him, so close he could feel the energy rising off her. "So what does that mean?"

Pulling a fortifying breath into his lungs, he turned to face her.

She stood not a foot away, her bare feet planted in the carpet, her arms crossed, mounding her breasts under the T-shirt. Her eyes seemed to sparkle with intensity, like Lake Michigan on a sun-drenched day.

The sight of her inspired a physical ache in his chest. "It means Hutch is out of our hair for the time being. It also means we're getting closer to catching the SOB."

"So what happens next?"

"I'm going to do a little investigating."

He didn't think it was possible, but her eyes brightened even more. "Investigating?"

"Trying to find out who is feeding Hutch information and providing him with your key."

"I'll go with you."

He shook his head. "It's safer if you stay here."

"You said Hutch was in Wisconsin."

"The Solar Sons are in Wisconsin. There's no telling if Hutch is with them."

"But he likely is."

He nodded grudgingly.

"So take me with you. I can help. I'm going crazy, Law. I've been in prison for months. First in the Solar Sons compound and now here. I've got to get out of this place."

He could understand the feeling. Though his need to escape was fueled more by sweet torture than a feeling of incarceration. And she had a point about her ability to help. Caroline knew these people. She could give insights he might not come up with on his own.

"Please, Law. You'll be with me. I'll be as safe as I am here. I've got to do something to help. I can't just sit around and be a victim any longer. I'll lose my mind."

Law blew an exasperated breath through tight lips.

"We'll stop at your lab first. I want to have a chat with Sophie."

"Today is Jimmy's first day back. It'll be good to see him."

Jimmy. He should have guessed. Caroline had been pressing since the fire to visit him, first at the hospital, then at his apartment. But with Hutch who-knew-where, Jimmy would have been too easy for the cult leader to stake out. Law hadn't allowed it. And though he knew damn well it had nothing to do with safety concerns, he wished he had reason not to allow it now.

Hell, he was as bad as Sophie.

Another worry tightened the back of Law's neck. "Being in the same room where Hutch tried to kill you might be tough. Are you sure you want to do this?"

Caroline straightened her spine. "I can't run from Hutch forever. I survived being a mile outside the Solar Sons compound. I can survive the lab at Quantum."

He had no doubt she could. She'd changed since the night she'd first faced Hutch's lies. She'd grown stronger, more sure of herself with every day that passed. It showed in the passion and vitality with which she attacked everything from reading the newspaper to beating him in chess. She was returning to her old self, the Caroline he'd known five years ago. The Caroline who infused everything in her life with passion and vitality.

And making love had certainly not been the exception.

He swallowed hard and pushed that thought as far from his mind as he could. "All right. We'll go this afternoon."

A spark of victory kindled in her eyes. "I'll be ready."

CAROLINE FELT anything but ready as the elevator carrying her and Law to the fifteenth floor of the Quantum Building slid open. Her heart seemed to flutter unevenly in her chest, and she was so out of breath it was as if she'd climbed the stairs to the fifteenth floor instead of merely riding the elevator. She had the urge to punch the button for another floor and let the elevator whisk her as far from her lab as possible.

As if sensing her distress, Law placed a hand on the small of her back, urging her to step out into the hall.

His touch seeped through her blouse and warmed her skin. He was so steady, so strong. Everything she wasn't. And she stood still for a moment, soaking up the contact like a neglected houseplant long in need of water.

Finally she drew in a deep breath and forced her feet to move forward. Law followed. The heels of their shoes clicked on the granite floor and echoed down the empty hall. As they passed other labs, Caroline could see her colleagues immersed in their work. The pressure in her chest began to let up. This was her building, damn it. Her lab. Hutch didn't own it any more than he owned her. And today, she'd take it back from him. Reaching the door, she grasped the knob and pushed the door open.

The lab looked exactly as it had before the fire. The tile floor was spotless, the wooden side of the workbench showed no blistering, and the air smelled slightly medicinal, slightly sweet, no sign of the scent of accelerant and burning human flesh.

Caroline sighed audibly. So far, so good. Her pulse slowed.

Sophie sat at one of the computers, her back to them. Her hair was tied into its usual twist. Her fingers flew over the keyboard. She didn't seem to hear them enter.

"Hello, Sophie."

The woman's fingers froze. Grasping the mouse, she flipped the page on the screen before she turned to face Caroline and Law. She forced a smile to her lips. "Hello, Caroline. Back for good? Or are you just dropping in to crack the whip?"

Caroline said nothing for a moment, stunned by her assistant's catty comment and the hard tone in her wispy voice. "I doubt there's a need for whip cracking, Sophie. You and Jimmy make a great team. I'm sure you're getting a lot done."

"Yes." Sophie dropped her gaze to the floor, as if she regretted her outburst. "It's nice having Jimmy back. I can't believe the whole thing about the fire. How did it happen?" She raised her eyes to Caroline once again. Then shifted her attention to Law.

"That's what we're here to find out." Law's voice was steady.

Sophie fidgeted her feet on the base of the chair.

"I don't know anything. I wasn't even here when it happened." She tilted her chin upward, as if daring them to accuse her of something.

"Did you see the package when it was delivered?" Law probed.

"Yes. But Jimmy accepted it."

Caroline looked around the lab for her other assistant. So Jimmy had received the package that ended up burning him. He should remember details of the exchange. He had as much at stake as she did. "Where is Jimmy?"

Sophie's lips tightened. "He's taking a break. He's not feeling well."

"Where is he? We need to talk to him." Law leveled a stern gaze on Sophie.

"I told him to take as much time as he needed." Sophie's lower jaw shot forward like a petulant child's. She gave Caroline a pointed stare. "I'll tell him you were here."

Caroline shook her head. Law's observations were true. Sophie clearly didn't like her. She obviously had more at stake than a simple crush. Sophie was waging war. A war Caroline hadn't even known existed.

But even though she didn't like Caroline, that didn't mean she was working with Hutch. It didn't mean she'd helped the Solar Sons kidnap Caroline or attempt to burn her with the incendiary device.

"Caroline."

She looked in the direction of the voice.

Jimmy emerged from the back room, a smile stretching across his lips. He held out his arms to her in a request for a hug. "Did you come to welcome me back?"

Caroline crossed the distance in a few strides and stepped into his arms. She hugged him gently, feeling Sophie's glare stab into her back like a honed stiletto.

"We have a few questions for you, Jimmy." Law's voice rose from the other side of the room.

The smile dropped from Jimmy's lips. Suddenly his eyes appeared guarded, as if he didn't trust, or didn't like, Law. "What kind of questions?"

"About the package. Sophie says you accepted it when it was delivered."

"Yes, I did." He didn't even glance at Sophie, as if she wasn't worth a second thought.

Caroline turned so she could get a glimpse of Sophie.

Her assistant watched Jimmy, a bruised look circling her eyes. She definitely had it bad. And Jimmy didn't notice a thing. Caroline ached for her.

"How did the package arrive?" Law continued to fire questions. "Why didn't it go through the X-ray machine like all the other packages coming into the building?"

"The receptionist said a courier brought it to the front desk. After that, I assumed it went to the mail room and went through the X-ray machine with all the other packages. It was brought up with all the other mail." He looked at Caroline and smiled.

A weight descended on her shoulders. Apparently Law had been right about more than Sophie's dislike. He was right about Jimmy, as well. For as much as

Sophie mooned for Jimmy, Jimmy had the same feelings for Caroline.

"I'm sure the mail room wouldn't have sent it up here if they'd known it was so dangerous."

Caroline reached up to give Jimmy a reassuring pat on the shoulder, then thought better of it. She rested her hand on her hip. "I'm sure you're right."

"I'm just glad you weren't hurt."

Caroline gave him a shaky smile, then turned to Law. "We'd better get going and leave these two alone to work. With all that's happened, our research is far behind where it should be already."

Law nodded. Resting his hand on her back once again, he ushered her toward the door.

Caroline soaked in the feel of his hand. She could feel Sophie's cold stare accompanied by, she was sure, Jimmy's glare in Law's direction.

What a mess. She'd never felt so uncomfortable in her lab before. She'd worked side by side with Jimmy and Sophie for years both at the Quantum Building lab and at the larger research facility out in Calumet, but she'd never picked up on the vibes slinging around like ricocheting bullets. Had she been blind? Or merely too absorbed in her work to notice?

As soon as the door closed behind them, she exhaled a sigh. "Sophie really does hate me. And it seems she has reason to."

"But the question is, does she hate you enough to sell you out to Hutch?"

Caroline felt numb. She didn't know. She didn't seem to know anything anymore. And how did she think she could face Hutch when she couldn't even face the jealousy of her assistant?

"Don't worry about Sophie. I'll sic Andy on her. He's supposed to be released from the hospital tomorrow. He can use those computers of his to dig up anything about anybody. When he gets done with Sophie, we'll know everything there is to know." Law slipped an arm around her shoulders.

Warmth traveled through her veins and soothed her mind. "Like what?"

"Like what she does in her spare time, and what environmental causes she cares about."

Caroline leaned her head back against Law's solid shoulder. She might not be strong enough to get through this on her own, but with Law's help, she could make it.

At least, that's what she wanted to believe.

Chapter Eleven

Thanks to rush-hour traffic, it was evening before they reached Caroline's building in Lincoln Park. Law watched Caroline's hands tremble as she slipped her key in the lock on her apartment door and slid open the dead bolt.

He reached a hand toward her, then let it fall uselessly by his side. He couldn't comfort her. Not with words and certainly not with a touch. He could still feel the warmth of her skin through her thin cotton blouse when he'd rested his hand on her back at the laboratory. He could still see the distress in her eyes when she realized her assistant hated her enough to hurt her.

Law's touch had done little to comfort her and everything to remind him of the soft and supple woman beneath that thin cotton. An image he didn't need bombarding his resolve.

She pushed open the door and stepped into her apartment. Biting her bottom lip, her gaze darted around the room as if she expected Hutch to jump out from behind a chair or potted plant.

Law stepped into the apartment behind her. As

soon as he did, he was profoundly grateful he hadn't touched her as she unlocked the door. He'd been in her apartment less than a week ago. But memories of that night five years earlier still slammed into him with the force of a sledgehammer upside the head. Instead of lessening since their last visit to the apartment, the memory had taken on a life of its own, an intensity that threatened to steal his sanity. The silk of her skin as he peeled off her clothing. The taste of her kiss. The scent of her arousal, her passion. The thrill of joining with her, being part of her, possessing her.

He attempted to clear his thoughts and tried to slow his runaway pulse. He wanted Caroline, that much he had to admit. He wanted her with a power that frightened him. But that didn't mean he had to give in to that desire. He couldn't. She trusted him. She needed him to help her work her way through this nightmare, to help her reclaim her life. And this time, he'd give her what *she* needed. "If this is too much for one day, we can come back tomorrow."

"The sooner I confront the truth, the sooner we can find out what's really been going on. And the sooner I can get Hutch out of my life." Straightening her spine, she marched off in the direction of the bedroom.

Law followed. Her show of bravery didn't fool him for a moment. She was afraid. And after what she'd been through, she had every reason to be. But he'd be there with her, helping her through this, giving her what she needed, whether that be a shoulder to lean on or help digging the truth from what was shaping up to be a veritable mountain of lies.

When she reached the bedroom, she sucked in a deep breath before focusing on the bed. The spread was smooth, perfect, no trace of the note that had been waiting for her last time. And to Law's relief, Andy and Whitney had also done a thorough job of cleaning up the dusting powder they had used in the room to search for fingerprints. The room looked as clean and neat as if Caroline had tidied up before leaving for work this morning.

Her shoulders fell as she exhaled the breath she'd been holding.

"Not so bad?"

She turned to him, her face looking much softer, less tense than it had moments before. "I know it's silly of me to have to come back here just to see, but—"

"Not silly at all."

She gave a slightly embarrassed smile. "Well, thank you for indulging me."

"Anytime." He'd meant for the answer to be flip, casual, instead it rasped from his throat in a husky growl. Like a late-night invitation.

The tip of her tongue darted between her lips, moistening them to a glistening red. Her breasts rose and fell with her breathing.

Swallowing into a dry throat, Law pulled his gaze away. "Are there any things you'd like to take back to the safe house? I can give you a moment to pack."

Out of the corner of his eye, he could see her nod. "How long do you think I'll have to stay there?"

He shrugged, trying to convey an ease he didn't feel. "There's no telling. But if you forget anything, we can always come back."

She opened the closet door, pulled out a small bag and spread it open on the bed. Rifling through drawers and closet hangers, she tossed items into the bag. After a short trip to the bathroom for toiletries, she was ready to go.

Law took the small suitcase from her, his fingers brushing hers for a moment and sending his pulse racing once again. Clamping down on his overactive imagination, he gestured to the door. "I want to stop and chat with Mrs. Hansen on the way out."

Caroline cocked her head. "To find out why she was such a sound sleeper the night I was kidnapped?"

"Among other things." He pulled open the door, and they exited.

As Caroline pulled out her keys to slide the dead bolt back home, the door across the hall opened.

"Hello, Caroline," Mrs. Hansen called in a sing-song voice.

How about that? They didn't even have to knock on her door. Apparently Mrs. Hansen was busy listening to the comings and goings of the building as she always did. Save for one night last March. And when Hutch or one of his followers left the Solar Sons' calling card on the bed a few days ago.

Caroline forced a smile to her lips. She could never be anything less than utterly friendly to her neighbor—that was her nature. "Hello, Mrs. Hansen.

How are you today? You remember my friend, Lawson.''

The woman gave Law a quick nod, then turned to Caroline with the single-minded intensity of a child compelled to tell her story. ''You'll never guess who's in *my* apartment today.''

Caroline gave her a blank look. ''Who?''

She swung her door open wider. From the hallway, Law could see into the kitchen. The building's superintendent was up to his elbows in the garbage disposal, pulling out something that looked like green plastic hair.

Law nodded a greeting to the man. Unfortunately the search Whitney had done into Yashi's background had yielded few results. The man simply seemed to have moved to this country out of nowhere, landed the superintendent job for this building, and lived his quiet life. And in Law's book, there was nothing like the lack of a background and a quiet life to inspire suspicion.

Caroline gave Mrs. Hansen a cheery grin. ''I'm glad Yashi can finally fix your garbage disposal.''

Mrs. Hansen's smile grew wider. ''I have a whole list for him today. He's not getting away from me.''

Caroline laughed. ''Have fun.''

Mrs. Hansen shot her a dour look. ''This isn't fun, it's work.''

''Then get a lot of work done.'' Caroline's smile didn't fade. She had the tolerance of a saint.

''He certainly will get a lot of work done this time.''

Law stepped from behind Caroline before Mrs.

Hansen could shut her door. "Before you go back to your work, I'd like to ask you a few questions, Mrs. Hansen."

The woman eyed Law. Her self-righteous smile dissolved into a frown of suspicion. "Who are you again?"

Law jutted his hand toward her in an offer to shake. "I'm an attorney. I'm looking into the viability of filing a class-action suit against the security company in charge of this building. If I determine there are grounds to sue, you are more than welcome to attach your name to the suit."

"And what do I have to pay?"

"Nothing. My firm would take a percentage of the final settlement."

Mrs. Hansen's eyes gleamed. "What questions can I answer for you?"

Law knew that cover story would pique the woman's interest. Pique her interest, hell, she was nearly salivating. "I was wondering about a night last March. Specifically the night Caroline left her apartment."

"I remember the night. After that, I didn't see her until the two of you showed up a few days ago."

"You seem to be pretty aware of everything that goes on around here."

The woman eyed him as if she wasn't sure if that was a compliment or not. "I try to look out for my neighbors. But I never pry."

"Of course. Did you hear anything that night? The night Caroline left?"

She screwed up her forehead. "No. I don't believe I did. I slept like a baby."

"Do you usually sleep well?"

"I wouldn't say usually. There's so much noise in this building at all hours, it keeps a body awake."

"But you don't remember hearing noise that night?"

She shook her head.

Beside him, Law felt Caroline shuffle her feet on the low-napped carpet. "Are you sure, Mrs. Hansen? I wasn't exactly quiet."

"I'm sure. I didn't hear a thing. I didn't even know you'd left until you didn't show up for several days. Then of course, I figured out you went away. And that's why you left me that wonderful gift. A going-away present." She gave Caroline the kindest smile Law had seen cross those uptight lips.

Caroline raised a delicate eyebrow. "A gift? I didn't leave you a gift."

Now it was Mrs. Hansen's turn to look puzzled. "You didn't? Then who did? It was sitting outside my door the afternoon before you left."

Law's pulse picked up its pace. "What kind of gift?"

"A lovely box of chocolates. My weakness."

"Did you eat them?"

"Of course. I can't resist chocolate. I'm afraid I ate them all. And they were delicious." She turned her attention back to Caroline. "But if you didn't leave them for me, who did?"

Law had a few ideas. "So you ate the chocolates

and then slept like a baby that night? Doesn't chocolate tend to keep you awake?"

"It usually affects me that way. But not that night. They must have been very high-quality chocolates." She almost beamed remembering the gift. "Do you suppose I have an admirer who left them for me?"

Caroline shot Law a questioning look. "Probably."

"Hmm." Mrs. Hansen turned her eyes to the ceiling as if caught in a dream. "I wonder who it could be."

"If you find out, let me know," Caroline said. "Now we'd better leave you to all that work Yashi's doing for you."

The woman's face suddenly became serious. "Yes. I really have to be going."

After saying their goodbyes, Law and Caroline walked down the stairs and through the door. When they reached the outdoors, Caroline stopped dead. "Are you thinking the chocolate was drugged?"

"If it was, we have our answer about why your neighbor didn't hear anything the night you were kidnapped. Mrs. Hansen indulged herself, then had a long, peaceful nap."

"And you think Hutch left those chocolates for her?"

"I doubt it was a secret admirer," he said wryly.

"That means Hutch would have to know everything about not just me, but my neighbors."

"He did his research."

"But you don't get information like the fact that Mrs. Hansen is nosy and likes chocolate from computer records. Someone would have had to tell Hutch. Someone who knows everything about my life.'' Her voice rose, panic coloring her words. ''Do you think Sophie hates me that much?''

Against his better judgment, he rested his hand on the curve of her back. ''We don't know it's Sophie. But believe me, if it is, we'll find out.''

''And then what?''

''Then we'll use her to find Hutch.''

''Follow her?''

''And tap her phone. Whatever it takes. And then we'll put them all in prison for a good long time.''

She nodded, but Law could tell the prospect of shutting her assistant in prison didn't make her feel better. If anything, she looked as if she felt worse. ''It seems like I didn't know my own life very well, did I? Even before the Solar Sons kidnapped me, I couldn't tell truth from lies.''

He curved his hand around her hip, pulling her tight against him. Her body trembled from deep inside. He longed to wrap both arms around her, hold her close until the trembling stopped.

''One of my assistants is in love with me, the other hates me. My neighbor is either a hapless victim, or she's lying through her teeth. And I don't know what to think about my family and their business dealings.''

''Your family—''

She held up a hand to stop him. ''I know. They're the salt of the earth. But I can't accept that on face value. Not anymore.''

He didn't know what to say. Even as an attorney

for the competition, he'd never doubted the integrity of Caroline's father. Henry Van Buren was tough, but fair. He may have been a bit domineering as a father, but Law had never had any reason to believe he was anything less than honorable when it came to his business or his personal life. He rubbed his hand up and down Caroline's side, feeling the gentle swells and dips of her rib cage through the thin blouse.

She leaned against him, her body heat melding with his own. Craning her neck, she looked up at him, her eyes clear and intense as a bright summer sky. Her lips glistened, full and moist and soft. They parted slightly, inviting him to kiss, to taste.

He lowered his mouth to hers. Circling her waist with his other hand, he pulled her body tight against him. So delicate, so soft, so delicious.

She wrapped her arms around his neck and pulled him down to her, as if she couldn't get enough. As if she wanted him as much as he wanted her.

But no one could want that much. It was insane. Mindless. He edged his tongue into her mouth, tangling with her tongue, tasting heaven.

And it wasn't enough. A kiss could never be enough. He wanted her. Not just her body. Not just her heat and her passion. He wanted all of her. Her sweetness, her kindness, her incredible mind. Her heart and the warmth that radiated from her soul.

He ended the kiss and looked into her eyes once again. He wanted her more than he could say. Wanted her in his arms and in his bed. Wanted her beside him, touching him, talking to him, just being with him. Not for one night. Not for one month. But for as long as he lived.

She ran a finger along his jaw, her touch inspiring a mixture of heat and chills. "The only person I know I can rely on is you, Law. You're the only one I can trust completely."

A dagger stabbed into Law's chest and twisted. He forced his arms to release her and stepped away.

She followed him with her eyes, a myriad of questions poised on her lips.

He couldn't deal with questions right now. Hell, he couldn't deal with much of anything. He certainly couldn't explain why he couldn't hold her, kiss her, love her the way he wanted. He was having a hell of a time explaining that to himself.

He gestured to the long shadows. Clouds gathered over them, blotting what little light was left from the sky. In the distance, thunder rumbled. "It's getting dark. And it sounds like a storm is moving in. We'd better get back to the safe house." Walking to his sedan, he opened the passenger door and waited for her to climb inside.

CAROLINE FOLDED her arms over her chest and leaned back in the passenger seat. She forced her gaze to focus on the street ahead. Rain pattered the windshield and transformed the city street into a mosaic of blurred light and color. The tires of Law's car sloshed through puddles, the sound filling the car with a sound lonelier than the wail of a blues guitar.

She touched her fingertips to her lips. She could still taste Law's kiss, still feel the warmth and pressure of his lips on hers, still see the need in his eyes. A need to comfort her, true, but it had grown into something more, something deeper, more personal. He'd needed her as much as she needed him. To make him whole. To give his life meaning, identity, truth, everything she'd been searching for since he'd rescued her from that cornfield. He needed those things, too.

Things they could give to one another.

She watched the streetlights' watery glow wash over his face. That look of need was gone now, replaced by a chin clenched so hard, lines dug into the corners of his mouth. He focused his determined gaze on the road ahead. He didn't like showing his vulnerability. One hardly had to be conscious to sense that. He wrapped his need inside him like a punishment.

Like a penance.

"Why are you punishing yourself?"

The lines around his mouth deepened. His gaze shifted to her for a second and then returned to the road. "What do you mean?"

"In the Solutions office garage you mentioned your job with Chicago Confidential was your penance."

One minute stretched into the next. Wipers slapped across the windshield. Puddles hissed and splashed beneath tires. Finally he drew a breath and glanced at her again. "I used to be a prosecutor."

"I know. You told me you had just quit the state's attorney's office when I met you five years ago."

He nodded. The lonely beat of rain tapped on the car.

She watched his face, waited for him to go on.

Finally he drew in a breath. ''I was forced out.''

She raised an eyebrow. She knew whatever was behind this need for penance was painful for him, but she'd never imagined it would include being forced out of his job. He'd always given her the impression he gave his life for his work. Much the same way she always had. She couldn't imagine him being forced to quit. ''How? What happened?''

''I was blindsided. I never thought much of the state's attorney who was voted in back then. Apparently he felt the same way about me. When he was sworn in, it seems he had no further use for me. He demoted me to prosecuting the equivalent of jay-walkers. After dedicating six years of my life to the prosecutor's office, four of those years in homicide. He knew I couldn't stand around and let him do that to me.''

''So you quit.''

''That very day.'' He grimaced. His voice took on a bitter edge. ''I decided I'd look out for number one from then on. So I went to work for Petrol for a huge salary and limited hours. I bought a luxurious condo I never spend time in, a Rolex watch that runs the same as any other watch, and this car. And...'' He stared out the windshield. Shadows of raindrops moved over his face like the ghosts of tears.

''And?'' she prompted.

''And that's when I met you.''

"During Petrol's lawsuit against Quantum. And against me."

"Over your hydrogen-combustion engine patent." His mouth twisted into a mask of self-loathing that stole Caroline's breath. "I decided I'd look out for number one with you, too."

She thought back to that night. She remembered it vividly. Much more clearly than the shadowed, confused memories from the past four months. She'd met him when he'd deposed her for the case. She'd been attracted to him at once, and when the deposition ran long and he'd asked her if he could buy her a late dinner, she'd gladly accepted. They'd talked about everything except the case. The Cubs' disappointing season. Their mutual love of Chicago blues music. Her desire to be closer to her workaholic sister, Natalie. When he'd asked if she'd like to go to a local blues club to see a great band, she hadn't hesitated to say yes.

It had been a whirlwind of sensation. The sultry music full of longing and pain, the feel of his body swaying against hers. And when he'd kissed her, she'd known she was lost.

She'd invited him home. They'd been so carried away with passion and desire, they'd made love right there in the entryway of her apartment. Her first time.

She'd never forget.

But what she didn't remember was him "looking out for number one" that night. Not in any way. He was warm and generous and giving. So much so that she'd been shocked and more than a little crushed when he'd never called her in the weeks afterward.

"Is that why you didn't call me? Because you were looking out for number one?"

"I took advantage of you that night. You deserved music and flowers. You deserved a man who loved you. A man who would make your first time special. And I—"

"It was a wonderful night, Law. It was everything I could ask for."

"You deserved more. Much more." He glanced in the rearview mirror. "But that wasn't the worst of it. The worst of it was after. When I was so worried about stirring up a conflict of interest regarding the lawsuit that I didn't call. And I didn't return your call."

That had hurt her. Hurt? Who was she kidding? It had broken her heart. Law had been the only man she'd allowed herself to relate to, to be herself with, to break out of the straitjacket of her scientific life. When she'd never heard from him, she'd thought he was turned off by the real her. It wasn't until this past week that she realized that was not the case.

"I treated you like dirt all because I didn't want to offend the company that bought and paid for me." He made a left-hand turn.

She leaned against the turn and then straightened. "You didn't want to lose your job, like you had before."

He waved away her words, his face hard with anger. "Don't make excuses for me, damn it. What kind of man does that to a woman he cares about? What kind of man chooses money over that woman?"

A woman he cares about.

His words shook her like a clap of thunder. For a moment, she didn't want to think. She didn't want to analyze what he'd said and fit it into its proper scientific perspective. She only wanted to soak in his words and feel.

A woman he cares about.

He focused on the rearview mirror. Headlights behind highlighted his eyes. "I think someone's following us."

The urgency of his voice cut through her thoughts like a cold blade. "What?"

"Someone's following us. Hold on." He swerved hard to the right.

Caroline clutched the dash for support. She craned her neck, peering out the back window.

A set of headlights swung around the corner behind them. Tires screeched and skidded on wet asphalt.

Her heart pounded high in her chest. "Hutch?"

"I don't know who else it would be."

"But how would he know where to find us?"

"Damn good question. Maybe Sophie or Mrs. Hansen, or whoever the hell is giving him updates on your life, gave him a little phone call." He took another corner. This time the back of the car fishtailed on the wet pavement. He brought the vehicle under control and gunned the engine.

The set of headlights followed.

Caroline's pulse rumbled like the thunder raging in the storm outside. "Or he could have been staking out my apartment. Or Quantum."

Cutting across lanes, Law made a hard left. Tires screeched. The car skidded around the corner.

Caroline held on. She glanced over her shoulder just in time to see headlights. "He made the turn. We can't shake him. What do we do?"

"We find the nearest police station. We take him right to the cops' door." An intersection loomed ahead. The light turned from red to green. Law gunned the engine again.

Something red streaked from the side street and headed right for them. Caroline gasped. Another car. She opened her mouth to scream.

Law hit the brake. They skidded. Too late.

Steel crunched. Glass shattered. And Caroline's head snapped forward.

Chapter Twelve

Law struggled to open his eyes. His car's air bag draped from the steering wheel like a deflated balloon. He forced his head to clear. Details of the accident spun through his mind.

Beside him, Caroline leaned forward in her seat belt, covering her face with her hands. The passenger-side air bag hung limp in front of her.

He grasped her arm. "Caroline? Are you all right?"

She groaned and let her hands fall from her face. Her eyes met his. "The red car. We hit it."

"It hit us." If he wasn't mistaken, the car had actually *accelerated* into them. Law looked through the spider-cracked windshield. The hood of his car jutted up at a strange angle. And beyond its twisted blue steel, he could see a sliver of red. Unease crept up his spine. "Can you get out of the car?"

He heard Caroline fumbling with the door handle. "My door is stuck."

He tried his own door. It opened on the second try. "Slide across." Grasping Caroline's arm, he helped her. He half lifted her from the car and set her on her feet.

From outside the vehicle, they could see the damage much better. The red car was wrenched around the front of his car, its entire driver's side smashed into scrap metal.

Caroline's eyes grew wide when she saw the damage. "Do you think the other driver is—"

The bent driver's door of the red car opened partway. A curse spit into the night.

Law could feel Caroline stiffen next to him. He didn't have to see the driver to know who was piloting that red car. Caroline's reaction to his voice said it all. "Let's get out of here."

Law grasped Caroline's arm and ran across the intersection. If Hutch was in the red car, he would bet Pike or another heavily armed member of Hutch's Solar Guard was in the car following them. Either way, he wasn't going to hang around to find out. As much as Law liked his Glock, it was no match for a machine pistol.

Law grabbed his gun from his shoulder holster as they ran. If they were lucky, the damage to Hutch's car would keep him trapped for a while. At least long enough for them to disappear.

Circling the corner, they raced in the direction of the river. Their shoes clacked on concrete. Rain pelted their faces, and puddles splashed their legs.

Cars drove past, drivers craning their necks to see what the commotion was about. But no one stopped to help. He couldn't blame them. They'd have to be crazy to stop for people running and brandishing guns. Their only hope was for a police cruiser to make its way down the street. A stroke of luck they couldn't afford to bet on.

It was up to him. He had to find a way to save Caroline. And himself.

They reached the bridge. The Chicago River wound below like a snake in the night. Instead of running forward onto the bridge, Law swung around the corner of a building and stopped dead. "We can't take the bridge. We'll be sitting ducks."

Caroline stopped beside him. She stared straight ahead, as if she didn't hear him. At first he thought she might be dissociating as she had during other stressful times. But then she raised her hand and pointed. "The scaffolding. On that building."

He followed the direction of her extended finger. Scaffolding used for restoration stretched along the lower floor of the building ahead. About eight feet off the ground, the steel tubes and wood planks stretched along the building's facade and turned the next corner.

"If we could reach a point where they couldn't see us and climb on top…"

She didn't have to elaborate. He grabbed her hand. They ducked around the corner and plunged into the shadows underneath the scaffold.

Rain pattered on the planks above, mixing with the rhythm of their feet on concrete. They reached the end of the planks. Stopping dead, they turned and looked up. Rain again assaulted their faces, stinging their cheeks and making it difficult to see.

Law bent down. Lacing his fingers, he lowered his hands so Caroline could step into them.

When she placed her foot into his hands, he lifted her up the steel frame. She grasped the tubing and hoisted herself onto the scaffold.

Law grabbed the rain-slick steel. Blinking against the driving rain, he pulled himself up on the scaffolding. His grip slipped then caught. Caroline's hands closed over his shoulders and pulled. He landed on the planks with a thump that blended with a roll of thunder from the sky.

The sound of running footsteps echoed underneath the scaffolding. The footfalls drew nearer and rounded the corner.

Law held his breath. If Hutch and Pike had seen his dangling legs when they turned the corner, they would know where to look. He clutched his Glock in his hand, its steel slick with rain. His lungs ached for air. The moment a face peeked over the scaffolding's edge, he'd be ready to fire.

Beside him, Caroline lay still as death. Her wide eyes met his.

"What the hell?" a voice shouted from below.

"Where are they?" Hutch shouted. "Did they get inside?"

A door handle rattled just below the planks.

Law's pulse pounded in his ears, loud enough to drown out the thunder.

"Down here. They must have headed for the river."

Footfalls followed the shout.

Craning his neck, Law peered over the edge of the

scaffolding. The outline of two men was barely visible in the driving rain. Only Hutch and Pike. No others. They ran around the corner of the building.

"What do we do now?" Caroline's voice trembled.

He turned back to her. Her face was pale, but her eyes held his. Firm. In control. She was scared, but ready to move.

"We wait a couple more seconds and then head back the way we came. Stay on the scaffold until we make it around the corner of the building."

"And then we go back to the car?"

"We can't do that. Too dangerous. Besides I doubt the car is in operating condition. We'll have to walk and find another place to stay."

"We can't go back to the safe house? Why?"

"That red car wasn't following us."

She gave him a questioning look.

"Pike was following us in the blue sedan. Hutch wasn't. Hutch was waiting."

"In the neighborhood of the safe house," she finished for him. Her lips thinned into a bloodless line. "So he knows where the safe house is, too."

"Maybe. Maybe not. But we can't take the chance."

"He knows." She stared into the rain-spattered night, her eyes taking on that hollow stare. "Hutch knows everything about me. And he won't stop coming after me. If I can't be part of his cult, if I can't be his, he won't stop. Not until I'm destroyed. Or dead."

Law reached for her, smoothing a wet strand of

hair from her cheeks. She looked so small and lonely lying there, freckled cheek resting on the wooden plank, rain soaking her to the skin. He wanted to wrap her in his arms and never let her go. "Hutch will stop, Caroline. He'll stop, because I'm going to stop him."

She looked into his eyes, the lines etched in her forehead lightening. "You will, won't you?"

"Yes."

"Your penance?"

He shook his head. "My pleasure."

A smile lifted the corners of her lips.

The sight of her smile hit him square in the chest. God she was beautiful. And strong. Stronger than she would ever know. Not many people could smile after what she'd been through. Not many people could find the courage to go on. But she could. She had more courage than anyone he'd ever known.

Most notably, himself.

But being around her, witnessing her rain-soaked smile, her determined voice, the spark of courage in her eyes made him want to be a better man.

"Time to go." Law rose to his feet. Caroline followed. Half running, half creeping, they moved along the wooden planks, back in the direction they came.

LAW LOOKED AROUND the simple decor of the hotel room. A generic painting of generic flowers hung on the wall. A standard table and two chairs found in every hotel room across the country huddled near the window. A pink-and-green print bedspread stretched across the king-size pedestal bed. The ordinariness was reassuring, comforting. All of it, except the sight of the bed.

The *one* bed.

He looked at Caroline, careful to keep his eyes glued to hers and away from her rain-soaked blouse conforming to each dip and curve, her nipples peaking with chill. "You can take the bed. I'll take a chair and watch the door."

Her eyebrows arched. "You expect me to sleep while you stand guard over me?"

"It won't do any good for both of us to go without sleep." It was common sense. Surely she could see that.

She wrapped her arms around her middle, pressing her breasts against the wet fabric, pushing her nipples into starker relief. "Can I ask you something?"

"Of course." Anything to get his mind off her body and that bed just a few feet away.

"In the car before the crash, you said you cared about me five years ago. Is that true now?"

Her question blindsided him. He looked into the eyes that were watching him, so honest, so open. It was time for him to be honest, as well. "Yes. If anything, I care more. But—"

"But what?"

"But I'm not the man for you. I can't give you what you deserve."

"Maybe not. I'm not sure what you think I deserve. But I do think you can give me what I need."

"What you need?"

Swallowing hard, she nodded. "When I was in the Solar Sons compound, Hutch used to tell me that once I proved myself loyal, he intended to take me into his bed.''

Law clenched his teeth. The thought of Hutch Greely anywhere near Caroline made his blood burn. ''Did he touch you?''

''No. He said I had to be worthy first. I had to forget all other men. I had to banish impure thoughts.''

Anger roiled in Law's gut.

''But I couldn't. I didn't want to.''

She had said that before. When he'd been deprogramming her. When she'd first started questioning Hutch's ''truths.''

''I didn't want to forget because the night with you five years ago was the most wonderful night of my life.'' She held up a hand to stay his protest. ''I know you think I deserved more. But believe me, I got everything I wanted. Everything.''

He wanted to believe her. He wanted to just forget the past, forget what he was and take her into his arms. Right here. Right now.

But he couldn't let himself do that. ''I don't want to hurt you again.''

''You won't hurt me, Law.''

''How can you say that?''

''I know you. You risked your life to save me from the Solar Sons compound, even when I didn't want to be saved. You showed me the truth. You protected me from Hutch. You helped me regain my life.'' She grasped his arms, forcing him to look into her eyes. ''You made me feel again, Law. You saved me. That isn't someone who will hurt me. That's someone who can love me. If he allows himself."

If he allows himself. Was it that easy? Did he merely have to give himself permission to want her, to love her, and then everything would magically work itself out?

It couldn't be that easy. If it were, she would have been in his arms long ago. Because it seemed he'd loved her from the moment they'd met.

"I need you, Law. I need you to help me."

"Help you? How?"

She unfolded her arms. Raising her hands to her throat, she slipped buttons from holes until her blouse gaped open, exposing a thin bra. The dark pink shadows of her nipples were easily visible through the wet cotton.

Law groaned under his breath. Heat surged to his groin.

Taking a step closer, she slipped the blouse off her shoulders and let it fall to the floor. "Hutch has infiltrated every part of my life. He enters my apartment at will. He may have turned my assistant against me. He seems to know my every movement. But he's never reached my heart. He's never been able to destroy what is between us. And I need that now."

He opened his mouth to protest, then clenched his teeth tight.

"I need you, Law." Reaching behind her back, she unclasped her bra. She shrugged the straps off her shoulders and let it fall. She stood in front of him, naked to the waist. Her breasts hung full and ripe, her nipples hard.

Suddenly he was beside her, touching her, kissing her. She felt so good. So right. As though she belonged with him. Right here, in his arms. In his bed. As though all the years and guilt and pain separating them had drifted away like storm clouds, and all that was left were the two of them and the clear night air.

She circled his neck with her arms, pressing her body close. Her lips were soft and sweet. Hunger bolted through him. He deepened the kiss, his tongue penetrating her mouth. She met his hunger with her own. Her tongue curled around his, teasing, stroking.

He wanted more. He needed more. He wanted to pick her up in his arms, to carry her to the bed, and bury himself inside her. Just as he had five years ago. Just as he'd wanted to do every day since.

He pulled his lips from hers and sucked in a breath.

"What's wrong?" She looked up at him, uncertainty bruising her eyes.

He smoothed a strand of damp hair away from her cheek. "You deserve more. You deserve flowers and music. Romance and candlelight. Not some bland hotel room. Not a hard bed or an even harder wall."

A smile tweaked the corners of lush lips. She was laughing. At him.

But her laugh didn't dim his determination. She did deserve more. And as hokey as it might be, he wanted to give it to her. He glanced around the bland room. He didn't have much to work with, but he'd do his best. Grasping her hand, he pulled her over to the bed. "Sit."

She tossed him an amused frown.

"Sit."

She sat.

He reached for the radio on the bedside table. Switching it on, he tuned the frequency until the slow grind of a blues guitar filled the room. "Music."

The music brought back that night all those years ago. The feel of her hips pressing against his, swaying as one to a grinding guitar. Heat pounded through him.

Holding her gaze, he gestured to the pictures on the wall above the bed. "These will have to do for flowers. They're pretty generic and don't have a fragrance, but—"

"They're lovely."

He smiled. She was something else. "Candlelight. We still need candlelight." He flicked off the light in the room. Rounding the bed, he walked to the window, grasped the curtains and yanked them open. The lights from nearby buildings twinkled in the rain, filling the window with glistening light. He turned back to face her.

Even in the darkness, her face eclipsed the light from layer upon layer of buildings behind him. "Better than candlelight."

He sat on the edge of the bed and reached for her. They fell onto the bed in one another's arms.

Law took her lips in a deep kiss. Urgency flooded his bloodstream, but he resisted. He would take his time. He would explore every part of her, indulge in every sensation. It would be different this time. She deserved the world. And this time, he'd give it to her. Leaning down, he littered kisses over her collarbone.

A small moan sounded deep in her throat, like the purr of a cat.

Need surged through Law's blood. He took her breasts in his hands, feeling their weight, their softness. Her nipples puckered, as if begging him to take them into his mouth. He brushed his lips over her skin until he reached her breasts. He circled a nipple with his tongue.

She drew in a sharp breath. Her fingers laced through his hair. She threw her head back and closed her eyes.

Heat built inside him. Need. He suckled her, delighting in her taste, her scent, the satin smoothness of her skin. He lingered over her nipples, her breasts, lavishing attention first on one and then the other.

She moaned and wriggled under him. Her fingers found the buttons of his shirt. Pulling them free, she clawed his shirt off his shoulders until their bare skin touched.

He moved down her belly, kissing her along the way. When he reached her jeans, he unfastened them and pushed them down her legs.

She arched her back, helping him slip the jeans down. Her fingers clawed at her silk panties.

Law slipped them off next, chasing the delicate fabric with kisses.

He kissed and tasted and loved her until she

begged for release. Only then did he slip off his own pants.

She leaned back and opened her thighs, accepting him. Slowly, gently, he eased inside, sinking into her warmth. Moving together, the heat and pressure built again, surging inside him, sweeping him away. And for the first time, he knew what it was like to belong with someone.

Because more than anything, he wanted to believe he belonged with Caroline. Heart, body and soul.

Chapter Thirteen

Caroline watched Law walk across the room away from her. Sunlight streamed through the window, turning his naked skin into alabaster, highlighting his broad shoulders, tight waist, firm buttocks.

She smiled in appreciation as the bathroom door closed behind him. With the drapes wide open, they'd awakened with the first light of dawn peeking through the buildings. They'd showered together, their attempt at cleaning up quickly soaring into another delicious round of lovemaking.

She hoisted her sore muscles off the mattress. If only they could stay in bed for hours, days, months. But that was impossible. Hutch was out there in the city, looking for her. And she would never be free of him until he was caught.

She found her clothing draped over a chair, the way Law had arranged them to make sure they would dry. Her lips curved into another smile. He was taking care of her again. Just as he had since he'd rescued her from the Solar Sons compound. Just as he had when they'd run from Hutch and Pike in the driving rain.

And just as he had in bed last night and again this morning.

She could still feel the kisses he'd scattered all over her body, so loving, so caring. He'd erased Hutch's conditioning all right. And he'd replaced it with images and feelings far more powerful.

She loved Law Davies.

The thought zinged into her mind like a lightning bolt, its aftermath sluicing over her like a warm rain. There was no use in fighting it. She loved Law. And with him by her side, Hutch Greely lost his power.

She pulled on her clothes just as the bathroom door opened. Law strode out, his clothing looking as wrinkled as his forehead, as if by putting them on, he had also donned his worries. "The bathroom's yours."

A shiver of fear peppered her skin. Five years ago after they'd spent the night together, he'd withdrawn. She knew he'd had his reasons. He'd explained them last night. And those reasons didn't exist now. There was no lawsuit. There was no conflict of interest. But she couldn't shake the fear that this night would turn out the same way.

She forced her feet to carry her across the floor. Stopping in front of him, she looped her arms around his neck and pressed her lips to his.

His lips softened under hers. He circled her with his arms, drawing her tight against him, devouring her kiss like a man dying of hunger.

Warmth seeped into her. She needn't have worried. Whatever his worries of Hutch and concerns about the day ahead, he wasn't withdrawing from her. He was there for her.

And with him by her side, she could overcome anything.

She ended the kiss and looked into his eyes. "So what is the plan for today?"

"We grab some breakfast, and then we start snooping into some people's lives."

"What about your car?"

"Vincent recovered it last night. He had it towed to the Solutions garage."

"It has my suitcase in it. The stuff I picked up at my apartment last night." She looked down at her blouse. The fabric looked as if it had spent a month in the bottom of a hamper. "I'd like to change."

"We'll make that our first stop."

A short taxi ride later, they were at the foot of the Langston Building. They took the elevator to a cove at the very bottom floor of the underground parking garage. A wide sliding door barred their way. Law stepped up to a small screen at the side of the door. Looking straight into the screen, he placed his fingertips on the pad below.

A red laser moved slowly across his face. When the laser had finished its trek, the door slid open.

She'd seen the laser scanner on her only other trip to the garage, the day they'd left for Hutch's compound, but it still amazed her. Everything about Law's double life amazed her. She followed him into the garage.

It didn't take long to spot Law's car. Grill smashed in, the car was twisted as if it had been through a crusher. Everything but the passenger compartment seemed dented and bashed.

Caroline swallowed hard. "It's a good thing we were wearing our seat belts."

"The passenger compartment is reinforced. Otherwise, being hit in front as well as behind... I don't know what would have happened."

She didn't want to think about it.

"It's a good thing I put your suitcase in the back seat instead of the trunk, or your clothes would be even more wrinkled than the blouse you're wearing." He opened the driver's door and reached into the car. He pulled out her jacket and handed it to her before ducking into the back seat for her suitcase.

The day was too warm for a jacket. Besides, with Law at her side, she was anything but cold. She draped the jacket over her forearm.

Something fell from the pocket and skittered across the ground.

Law set her suitcase down, his eyes following the sound. "What's that?"

Caroline ran her gaze over the concrete floor. "I don't know."

Law searched the floor with her. Finally he knelt and picked something up. He held out his hand. The button she'd found on her dresser perched between his fingers, the red cross nearly glowing against the blue background in the parking garage's dim light. "Yours?"

"I found it in my bedroom the first time we went to my apartment. I slipped it in my coat pocket."

Law turned it over in his fingers. "The flag of Iceland, right?"

She nodded. "I think it might be Natalie's. She had an Icelandic wool sweater with buttons like that. All the Quantum executives had one. Maybe the button fell off and my mother put it up on the dresser when she was watering my plants and tidying up." It was plausible. Her mother was always tidying up, even when Caroline didn't want her to.

He raised an eyebrow. "When was the last time Natalie wore that sweater to your apartment?"

She searched her memory. She didn't have a clue. "Quite a while ago. I haven't seen her wear it for maybe a year."

"And a button suddenly shows up in your apartment? That seems odd."

He was right. It was odd.

He rolled the button in his fingers, studying it carefully. "It looks like it was torn or cut. Some of the fabric is still attached."

A picture flashed in Caroline's mind. An image that chilled her to the bone. Maybe she'd been wrong. Maybe the sweater wasn't Natalie's. "Yashi has a gray wool cardigan. He wore it all last winter. Maybe the button is his."

Law's gaze riveted to hers. "Does his sweater have the same buttons?"

"I don't know. I've never noticed the buttons." Her mind raced ahead. "But it could have been ripped off his sweater when he was fixing something in my apartment, and my mom set it on the dresser in my bedroom."

"Or it could have been ripped off when he was helping the Solar Sons subdue you."

She forced herself to acknowledge the thought she didn't want to put into words. "But you said Whitney didn't find anything to tie Yashi to the Solar Sons."

"That doesn't mean nothing is there. We just can't find anything through the usual means."

Memories of the many times Yashi came into her apartment under the ruse of fixing things shot through her mind. Times when the two of them were in the apartment alone. Her nerves vibrated like piano wire. "So what do we do?"

"We use unusual means." He offered her a reassuring smile and ran a hand down her arm. "We'll get him, Caroline. And we'll get Greely, too. Everything's going to be okay."

She moved close to him.

He circled an arm around her shoulders and held her. His warmth seeped through her wrinkled blouse and wrapped around her heart.

She believed him. As long as she was with Law, tucked against his side, she could handle anything. Everything truly would be okay.

She looked over the twisted metal in front of them. Inside on the driver's seat, an envelope caught her eye. "What's that?"

Law followed her gaze. "What the hell?" He stepped to the window and grabbed the envelope. He opened it and pulled out a letter. Slipping on his reading glasses, he scrutinized the type. All blood seemed to drain from his face.

Caroline's stomach tightened. "What is it?"

He folded the paper and slipped it and the envelope into his pocket. Picking up her suitcase from the garage floor, he stepped toward the door they'd entered.

Caroline ran after him, grasping his arm to stop him. "Tell me, Law. What is it?"

He stopped and turned to face her. His face was nearly colorless. "I'm sorry, Caroline. I—" He held out the paper to her, his hand shaking.

She slipped it from his fingers and unfolded it. A letter stared back at her, written on Petrol Corporation's letterhead and addressed to her father. She read the type, a cold emptiness sinking into the pit of her stomach.

The plan the letter outlined was a familiar one. She'd read the words before. Hutch had shown a copy to her, a copy without the letterhead. He'd made her read every word out loud until she could recite them in her sleep. But there was one difference. Hutch had told her the letter had originated within Quantum. He'd lied. The plan to gain control of her research and bury it, the plan to hide her hydrogen-combustion engine in order to protect oil profits, the plan she held in her hands, hadn't come from Quantum Industries. It had come from Petrol.

No doubt Hutch had left the letter in Law's car after he'd rammed into them last night. No doubt he wanted to show her that Petrol had come up with the plan. Because Law was part of Petrol.

She looked up from the paper and searched Law's

eyes. "When you sued Quantum and me for the patent, you wanted to bury it all along."

"That's how it appears."

She thought of his shock when he'd found the letter in his car, the way the blood drained from his face. "But you didn't know about it."

"I should have."

"But you didn't," she said, her voice emphatic. "You didn't know."

He shook his head.

She wanted to wrap her arms around him, kiss the tortured look from his face, reassure him that everything was okay, that nothing had changed. But she knew it would be no use. He wouldn't accept her touch, her kiss. Everything had changed.

"I should have known, Caroline."

"Maybe they didn't want you to know. Maybe—"

"No. I didn't know because I chose not to know. I didn't want anything to ruin my promising career with Petrol. I was too busy looking out for number one."

The bitterness in his voice scared her. "No, Law, you wouldn't—"

"How can you say I wouldn't? I *did.*"

"Maybe you did. So what? It was a long time ago. I think you've more than done your penance. This letter doesn't matter anymore. It doesn't have to change anything."

"It changes everything."

His words cut into Caroline like a sharp blade.

"I don't want to hurt you, Caroline. I hurt you before, and I can't let myself do it again."

"What are you saying?" Panic shrilled along her nerves. This couldn't be happening. He couldn't be saying this.

"God, Caroline. If I turned my back on this, what's to keep you from believing I didn't get involved with you five years ago with the express purpose of using you."

"You didn't."

"Do you *really* know that? I don't. The subconscious is a funny thing. If I could turn a blind eye to Petrol's true purpose for the lawsuit, can you really trust that I didn't get involved with you because I subconsciously wanted to use you?"

"That's ridiculous."

"Is it? The mind can justify anything. You should know that better than anyone after what you've been through."

"You're right. The mind can play tricks like that. It can justify any belief or type of behavior. God knows my mind did when I was with Hutch. But no amount of 'tricks of the mind' can change who a person is."

She sucked in a breath. She had to convince him. She had to make him understand. "You're a good man, Law. I've seen it in your actions as well as your words. You risked your life to save me from the cult. You helped me get my life back when you probably should have just shipped me off to my family. You saved Jimmy's life in the lab. You saved *my* life."

He shook his head as if none of the things she'd said redeemed his one mistake.

She balled her hands into fists. He had to listen to

her. He had to believe. "So you were selfish at one
point in your history. So what? Most people are
happy if there's one point in their lives where they
weren't selfish. You're a good man, Law. I wouldn't
love you if you weren't." She didn't realize what
she had said until the words hung in the air between
them.

His face froze. His gaze bore into her. "And that's
exactly why I can't be near you. I don't want to hurt
you again."

How could he be so blind? He had to see what
was between them, didn't he? He had to feel the
energy, the strength, the love when they were together, didn't he? He couldn't honestly think she was
better off without him. He couldn't honestly believe
he would only hurt her again. There had to be another answer, another reason for what he was doing.
"No. That's not it. That's not it at all."

His spine stiffened, as if he was bracing himself
for what would come next.

The pieces came together in her mind. "You
aren't running away from me, from us, in order to
protect me. You're running away because you're
scared."

Surprise lifted his eyebrows. "Scared?"

"You don't want to be let down. You gave your
all to the state's attorney's office, and they betrayed
you. You sacrificed your self-respect to work for Petrol, and now they've betrayed you, too. You don't
want to take a chance again. You don't want your
heart broken."

"That isn't true."

"Isn't it?"

He clenched his jaw. "No. I'm a bastard. Pure and simple. And I'm not going to take advantage of you again."

"You're afraid of throwing yourself over the cliff, trusting I will be there for you. You're afraid to take a leap of faith."

He paced across the concrete floor. "That's not the case here. The bottom line is that I'm not going to hurt you."

"You're hurting me now." He was. She felt as though her heart had been carved from her chest.

He reached a hand toward her, then let it fall to his side without making contact. Turning away from her, he strode the remaining steps to the exit and stopped in front of the door. "Go to your family, Caroline. Reconcile with them. They're the ones who love you. They're the ones who can help you. I'll take you to Natalie."

YOU'RE A GOOD MAN, *Law. I wouldn't love you if you weren't.*

Caroline's words rang in Law's ears as he watched the numbers flash over the elevator door. Her scent filled his senses. The soft sound of her breathing tickled his ear. She stood close enough for him to touch, to hold, to kiss. Just one movement and he could take her in his arms and pretend the memo burning a hole in his jacket pocket didn't exist.

He clasped his hands behind his back and focused on the numbers. How could he have let it come to this? How could he have let her fall in love with him?

How could he have let *himself* fall in love?

A cold sweat broke out on his palms. It was true. He did love Caroline. More than he'd loved anyone in his life.

He loved everything about her. The way her forehead creased when she was worried. The river of passion flowing beneath that scientific exterior. The generousness in her heart.

And God help him if he ever broke that heart.

The elevator door opened on the ground floor. Law stepped out first and waited for Caroline. Without a word he walked through the vestibule beside her and headed to the street to hail a cab.

The sooner he could get her to Quantum's secure office building and back in the arms of the family who loved her, the better. He'd promised himself he wouldn't hurt her this time. And although he was too late to spare her all pain, he still had to try to keep his promise. For himself as much as for her. Because he couldn't live with breaking her heart. Not this time.

Chapter Fourteen

Caroline walked across the lobby of the Quantum Building toward the first bank of elevators. She'd left Law at Quantum's door with a simple goodbye. She'd said everything she could to change his mind, to no avail. There was nothing left to say.

She swallowed into an aching throat. Last night had been the night of her dreams. Law had been so gentle, so attentive, so wonderful. The night only made the light of day more cruel.

She'd been kidnapped and brainwashed. She'd only recently begun feeling emotions other than guilt and shame. And Hutch had tried to kill her. She'd weathered it all. Until now.

Who knew it would be Law who would inflict the fatal blow?

The thought rested bitterly in her mind. Law's actions spoke to the type of man he really was. Why couldn't he see that? He wasn't a selfish sellout. He was the most self-sacrificing, generous, caring man she'd ever known. He'd proved that last night. He'd proved it every day since he came to the compound pretending he was her husband. And now, no matter what she said, she couldn't make him see it.

She reached the elevator and stepped inside. After scanning her identification, she paused, staring at the panel of numbers. Her finger hovered over the button for the fifteenth floor for a moment. What she wouldn't give to retreat to her lab for the night and lick her wounds. She drew a deep breath and pressed the button of a much higher floor. This time she couldn't run away. This time she had to face Natalie.

A myriad of emotions stirred inside her. Not the least of which was the wish that Law would go with her to lend her strength.

She chased away the thought and the bitterness that followed it. She would have to find the strength in herself. She would have to face Natalie on her own.

She smoothed a stray hair back from her face. She might be nervous about confronting her sister. She might be scared. But whatever the outcome of their meeting, she knew she could get through it. At least that was one thing that being with Law had taught her five years ago. She had the strength to go it alone. As miserable as she was without him, she could go on. And she'd prove it.

She'd be damned if she didn't.

Caroline stepped out of the elevator and walked down the hall to Natalie's office suite. After the secretary buzzed Natalie, she told Caroline to go right in.

Drawing a breath of courage, Caroline stepped into Natalie's office and closed the door behind her. She traveled the room with her gaze. Much different from the decor the last time Caroline had set foot inside these walls.

"Hello, Caroline." Natalie's rich voice filled the room. She stepped into the main office, professional as usual in a tailored business suit. "I'm glad you finally came to see me. I would have visited you, but Lawson advised against it."

So that's how Law had kept her family at bay. Instead of telling them she refused to see them, he'd merely advised against it, as Natalie put it. Caroline raked the room once again, not sure if she was ready to meet Natalie's eyes. "You've redecorated."

Natalie gave a short derisive laugh. "A bomb's idea. Not mine exactly."

Surprise jolted through Caroline's blood like a shot of espresso. "A bomb?" Despite herself, her gaze flew to Natalie. She looked as sophisticated and put together as she always did. Her shoulder-length hair was exquisitely cut. Her makeup flawless and her manner impeccable. The perfect picture of an ambitious female executive. With one difference.

Her eyes. Somehow Natalie's eyes seemed softer than Caroline remembered. And that softness was now filled with obvious worry for her sister. "It's a long story. Suffice it to say, no one was hurt. Just my office decor."

The sense of relief coursing through her surprised Caroline. Hutch had conditioned her to think of her sister as the enemy, yet standing in this room with Natalie, Caroline still felt a connection. Worry at the news of the bomb. Relief that neither she nor anyone else had been hurt.

"I was worried about you, Caroline. I never could quite believe that you'd join a group like the Solar Sons. No matter what the e-mails you wrote me said."

Caroline vaguely remembered writing e-mails to her sister. Scathing, condemning e-mails. Hutch had stood over her, declaring each word she was to type onto the screen, his eyes drilling into her if she so much as hesitated to copy the words he gave her. She dropped her gaze to the plush carpet under her feet. "I'm sorry about the e-mails."

Natalie waved away the apology. "I knew they didn't come from you. You never could have written those things about our parents, about me. You never could have felt that way."

"I did feel that way." Guilt lodged in her throat.

"But not on your own. Lawson filled me in on the way brainwashing works. And the horror you went through. I just want you to know I'm here for you." Natalie stepped around her desk, removing the obstacle between them. She opened her arms, asking for a hug.

Caroline ached to fall into Natalie's arms, to talk to her sister the way she used to when they were children, to cry until she had no tears left. But as much as she wanted everything to be right between them, she couldn't just blindly accept Natalie's embrace.

Not until no more secrets stood between them.

She gestured to one of the chairs in front of Natalie's desk. "May I sit down?"

The smile fell from Natalie's lips. She dropped her hands to her sides. "Certainly."

Caroline crossed to a chair and perched on the edge. "I need to talk to you about some things. Things regarding Quantum's policies. And I need you to be honest with me."

Natalie pursed her lips and nodded. Instead of fading back behind her desk, Natalie canted the other chair to face Caroline and sat, her knees inches from Caroline's own. "I'll tell you whatever you want to know."

"It's about the lawsuit Petrol Corporation brought against us five years ago."

Natalie's green gaze searched Caroline's face, as if trying to read her mind. "The one Lawson Davies headed up."

Caroline drew a deep breath at the third mention of Law's name. She couldn't let herself think of him. If she did, she'd probably start to cry. And she couldn't cry. Not now. She needed to go on with her life. And the most important part of that was discovering the truth about her family and their business dealings.

Her family and her work were all she had left.

"Petrol sent our father a letter. It stated that they would drop the suit if he agreed to bury the hydrogen-combustion engine I developed." She watched Natalie's face carefully. If her sister gave any sign she knew about the letter, any sign that she was covering for their father's or her own actions, the life Caroline struggled so hard to reclaim after Hutch's brainwashing would be gone. "They dropped the suit a week later."

Natalie's eyes widened. "And you think Dad agreed with their conditions?"

"Did he?"

Natalie reached toward Caroline and covered her hand with her own. "No. He couldn't have. Dad has always been your biggest supporter, Caroline. Unless you include Mom and me."

"How do I know that?"

"What do you mean how do you know that? Don't you remember all the money he allocated to your research? He built the entire research facility in Calumet for you so you would have room to test your engine in actual cars."

"And with your public-relations help, he used all of that to gain goodwill for the company."

"And that should prove his intentions right there, Caroline. Think about it. He encouraged you to write articles about your research in scientific journals. He even got you that article in *Time* magazine. If he were trying to sweep your research under the rug, why would he have been so public about it?"

The sincerity in Natalie's eyes and words seeped into Caroline's heart like rain after a long drought.

Natalie held out her hand. "All of us are behind you, Caroline. We believe in the work you're doing."

Caroline let out a sigh. So the plot was Petrol's alone. Her family members weren't the greedy liars Hutch had said they were—the enemies of the earth that she had believed. She grasped Natalie's hand and squeezed it tight. "I'm so sorry."

Natalie leaned forward and enfolded Caroline in her arms. "Welcome back, sis. I missed you."

"I missed you, too." Caroline swallowed hard, tears welling in her eyes.

Natalie pulled back from her. "I don't want to rush things, but how about Mom and Dad? They're so worried about you."

Caroline nodded. She needed to talk to her parents. She needed to set things straight with them, as well.

"How about dinner at the house tonight? I was going anyway. I think Dad wants to grill Quint about our wedding date."

"Quint? The cowboy who works with Law?"

Her smile grew until she was positively beaming. "One and the same."

"You're getting married?"

"As soon as we can throw together a society wedding to make Mom proud."

Caroline tried to envision the laid-back cowboy with her all-business sister. No wonder Natalie seemed softer, less driven. She'd *have* to change to fall in love with Quint Crawford.

"Congratulations, Natalie. Quint is a great guy. I'm so happy for you." She reached out her arms and hugged her sister, trying to ignore the empty ache that wrapped around her own heart.

"Thanks, Caroline. I've wanted to ask you if you'd be my maid of honor."

Caroline's eyes misted. "Of course. I would love to."

"I'm so glad. I couldn't imagine getting married

without you standing beside me.'' Natalie pulled back and looked into Caroline's eyes. ''And as maid of honor, your first job is to come to dinner tonight at Mom and Dad's. You can help take some of the heat off Quint and me.''

Tonight. Caroline's head whirled. She'd been through too much in the past twenty-four hours. She'd lost Law and she'd regained her sister. She couldn't face her parents tonight. She couldn't explain what she'd been through, and she couldn't deal with the inevitable questions. ''How about tomorrow night?''

''Certainly. I'll set it up.''

''Thanks.''

''What are sisters for?''

Caroline blew a relieved breath through pursed lips.

''Lawson said you aren't to leave the building until Quint gets here. He'll be protecting you until Hutch Greely is found. He'll be here soon. You're welcome to wait here with me.''

''You and Quint keep your dinner plans. I'm going to go down to the lab. Jimmy came back to work yesterday, and I want to start catching up on our work. Quint can pick me up later.''

''Work. Why am I not surprised? But do me a favor, Caroline.''

''What's that?''

''Don't invest your whole life in work.''

''That's funny coming from you.''

''I've learned a bit in the past few months. There's

more to life than work. Much more. And I want you to be as happy as I am.''

Caroline gave her sister a genuine smile. She hadn't lost her family. She wasn't alone in the world, no matter how desolate she felt. And maybe there was a chance she could pick up her life and move on. Without Law.

Her heart twisted at the thought of him. He was so certain he wasn't good for her. If only he knew how much he'd done for her. If only he believed in their love.

But he hadn't five years ago. And he didn't now. And all she could do was figure out a way to pick herself up and move on. Alone. And the least painful way to do that was to bury herself in her work.

LAW STEPPED OFF the elevator in the Langston Building and strode to the Solutions, Inc., office suite. It had been a hell of a long day. After he'd said good-bye to Caroline at the Quantum Building, he'd gone straight to Petrol. He'd had to wait several hours to see Petrol's CEO, but the look on the man's face when Law tossed the copy of his letter to Quantum had been worth the wait. Just as Law had expected, he'd shown no remorse for his proposal to bury Caroline's research. Nor had he made excuses for his actions. Petrol had to protect its profits. Pure and simple.

And Law's decision following the meeting had been pure and simple as well. He returned to his office and drafted his resignation. The CEO would get it in the morning.

He paused outside the glass doors leading to Solutions. The rest of his life was neither pure nor simple. In fact, it was a damn mess.

He'd thought of nothing and no one but Caroline all day. The scent of her body heated with passion, the music of her laughter, the look of betrayal in her eyes.

He'd been an idiot to ever think they had a chance. He knew better, but he'd ignored his gut. And as a result, he'd hurt her. Again. And now he would never forgive himself.

He raked a hand through his hair and tried to clear his mind. He couldn't think of Caroline. Of the passion, the love he'd tasted. Of the trust in her eyes when she'd looked at him, trust that was sorely misplaced. He had to put her out of his mind and concentrate on the things he could do to help her. The ways he could keep her safe.

Drawing a deep breath of resolve, he pushed open the doors and strode into the lobby of Solutions. What he saw stopped him in his tracks.

Kathy stood behind the reception desk, her back to the door. And standing in front of her, arms around her ample figure and lips claiming hers, was Liam Wallace.

Law closed his eyes. He and Caroline had been in a similar pose not eight hours ago. He could still feel the soft imprint of her lips on his. And now it was all over. He cleared his throat.

Kathy and Liam jumped apart. Face red, Kathy stammered, struggling to regain her bearings. "Lawson, I—"

"Didn't mean to interrupt anything."

"You didn't interrupt. Liam was just—" She stopped, obviously unsure how to explain what Liam was just doing. Her cheeks burned so red, Law felt her embarrassment from across the room.

Law held up a hand, waving away her explanations. "Is Vincent in? Or did he go home already?"

"He's inside with Whitney and Andy." Kathy looked at the floor, at the cherry reception desk, at Law's shoulder, anywhere but at him.

Liam stepped toward Law. "None of this is Kathy's fault. I can explain."

"Don't worry about it." Law stepped past the two of them and toward the hallway leading to the Solutions boardroom and the Chicago Confidential special-operations room beyond. "You don't have to explain. Kathy is so sweet that I think all of us have wanted to kiss her at one time or another. Even Whitney."

Liam gave him a grateful grin. Kathy just shook her head. Sinking into her chair, she buried her face in her hands.

Law glanced out the window on the way to the boardroom. Shadows stretched long over the steel-gray waves of the lake. Streetlights blinked on and headlights wound like a glittery snake along Lake Shore Drive. The city would be dark in minutes, and the loneliness of night closed around his throat. Loneliness that just last night he'd banished with Caroline's touch and soft kisses.

He shook those thoughts from his mind and headed for the special-operations room. He was torturing himself. Not that he didn't deserve it, but it didn't accomplish anything. It didn't make Caroline safe. It didn't catch Greely or find whoever was feeding the cult leader information about Caroline's whereabouts.

He entered the boardroom and completed the retinal scan. The door to special operations slid open.

Vincent, Whitney and Andy clustered together in the wide, windowless room, emptying a box of what looked like bomb parts and spreading them across an examination table. Vincent latched on to Law's gaze as soon as he entered the room. "Where have you been the past few hours?"

Vincent never asked his whereabouts. Something must be up. "At Petrol. Writing my letter of resignation. Why?"

"Your letter of resignation? Why the hell would you do that?"

Law clenched his jaw. The past few hours had been among the toughest of his life. He didn't want to go into it. Not with Vincent. Not with anyone. "Because I can't work for them anymore."

A dark cloud seemed to descend over Vincent.

Whitney laid a hand on his shoulder, as if to steady him. "You may not want to do that yet, Lawson."

"Why not?"

"The Middle Eastern terrorist case we've been working on seems to be heating up. It may be helpful to have someone inside the big oil companies. We have Henry Van Buren's and Natalie's cooperation, but we don't have anyone inside Petrol except you."

Since he'd rescued Caroline, he hadn't had much

of a role in the investigation into the terrorist plot against Quantum. He'd been too busy protecting Caroline and trying to put Greely out of business. He mentally switched gears. "What happened with the case? Don't tell me there was another attack on Quantum's holdings."

"No. Not yet anyway." Vincent leveled him with a serious glare. "As you know, we suspect a connection between Zahir and Al-Sayed. A close connection. We have definite proof that Zahir Haji Haleem is betrothed to Al-Sayed's daughter."

Whitney piped up. "Miah Mohairbi. She was smuggled out of the Middle East and adopted and raised by a family in Chicago. Apparently before she was given up for adoption, she was betrothed to Zahir."

Law couldn't imagine someone's life being determined for her when she was only an infant. "But she's an American now. Do you really think she's going to go along with this betrothal?"

"Apparently, yes. Plans seem to be moving forward."

The meaning of this sunk into Law's mind. He shot Vincent a probing look. "And Javid?" The prince of the peaceful country of Amad, Javid was currently working with Chicago Confidential in an attempt to bring down the terrorist network. At the moment, he was undercover, pretending to be his twin, Zahir. "Is he planning to pose as Zahir for the wedding, too?"

"I haven't talked to him about it yet. But if we want to get to the bottom of this terrorist plot against

Quantum, we need a man on the inside. He's in the ideal position.''

Law had to agree, though the moral implications of entering into a marriage posing as someone else ate at him.

"So we need to know what's going on with the oil companies as all these plans come to a head." Whitney chimed in for the knockout punch.

Law let out a defeated sigh. "All right. I talked to the CEO, but I didn't officially resign. I'll have my assistant hold up the letter. But as soon as we nail Al-Sayed and destroy his terrorist network, I'm done at Petrol." He set his jaw. Delaying his resignation was bad enough. He wasn't going to let Vincent talk him out of it. After the letter he'd found, he couldn't work for Petrol. He had enough to feel guilty about.

"I heard you gave Quint the job of watching Caroline Van Buren. Care to fill me in?"

Law shifted, uncomfortable in his own skin. "She agreed to talk to her sister. Since Quint was stopping by to see Natalie anyway, I figured he could pick her up afterward and take her to her parents' house."

"But she didn't go to her parents' house," Vincent said.

Law raised his eyebrows, but he wasn't surprised. Caroline still had a lot to sort through where her parents and the company were concerned. He was hoping she could reconcile her feelings. He was hoping she could cleave to her family so she wouldn't be all alone in the world. "So the meeting with Natalie didn't go well?"

"Natalie said it went well," Whitney explained.

"Caroline just wasn't ready to face her parents, too. She didn't feel up to explaining things."

Law could imagine. How did one explain being brainwashed to turn against one's family? Worry wound in the pit of his stomach. "So where is she now?" he asked Whitney.

"At Quantum. Natalie said she wanted to catch up on some work."

He exhaled a breath he didn't realize he was holding. "Are you sure she'll stay at Quantum? The security there is tighter than at the White House. But if she steps outside, she might be in danger."

"She can't stay there all night. Someone will have to pick her up." Vincent gave Law a pointed look.

The knot reformed. Knowing Caroline and how he'd left her this afternoon, she probably would prefer spending the night in her lab with her buddy, Jimmy, than going anywhere with him. "So you want me to do it?"

"Is there a reason you shouldn't?"

Law hesitated. He'd rather work the rest of his life stealing patents at Petrol than spend one more night within the same walls as Caroline. He'd hurt her enough already. Seeing him again would probably be torture for her. It sure as hell would be torture for him. He met Whitney's eyes. "Maybe you could take her someplace safe. I don't think she wants to see me tonight."

Whitney raised a delicate eyebrow. Finally she nodded. "I'll pick her up. She can stay in our guest room. Just until we are sure the safe house hasn't been compromised."

Silence hung in the air like a bad smell, finally Vincent gave a nod. "Fine. I'll walk you to the garage." Picking up his computer and a briefcase full of papers, he tossed a last look to Andy. "Dexter? You leaving?"

Andy hunched over a magnifying glass, deep in contemplation over a small metal piece.

Law had to admit it was great to see Andy back at work. He seemed like the same loopy scientist he was before he'd been beaten to a pulp by the Solar Sons, albeit a bit more quiet.

"Dexter?" Vincent's voice held its usual note of impatience.

Andy finally looked up. "I'm going to stay here awhile."

Vincent finally turned his gaze on Law. His forehead darkened. "Are you staying, too, Law?"

Law met his gaze. "I'll help Andy."

Vincent spun on his heel and headed for the door.

"Bye, fellas," Whitney said and followed her husband.

As soon as the door slid closed behind them, Law exhaled with relief. He forced his attention to the bomb pieces scattered on the table in front of them. "Pieces recovered from the Solar Sons compound?"

"Yup. Pieces of the incendiary device. Vincent and Whitney went over them before, but this is the first chance I've gotten to really look at them since I was released from the hospital."

"What did Vincent come up with?"

"Prints belonging to Greely and some of the other

members who have police records. And— Wait a second.''

''What? Do you see something?''

He nodded his curly blond head. ''Get a load of this.''

Law leaned close to the magnifying glass. He was ready to think about anything but Caroline. And a break in the case against Greely was just the ticket. ''What is it?''

''Some companies stamp their code on specialized components made by them.''

''So they can be identified? Why would they do that if they are building components for bombs?''

''Some of these parts aren't components for bombs. As slick as these little red babies look, they're homemade. Patched together from unrelated pieces into a nice little package by someone who knows what they're doing. The parts are collected from different things. Like this one, for instance.'' He held up a minuscule part. ''This is used in engines. Specialized combustion engines. There's no reason for the company to hide their identity when making a part like this.''

A bad feeling niggled at the back of Law's neck. ''And what company made the part?''

''See that little letter?'' Andy pointed to a small bump on the part.

Law slipped on his wire-rimmed reading glasses to get a better look. ''I can't make it out.''

''See the round shape with the little tail? It's a stylized *Q*. The symbol for Quantum Industries. Greely was using Quantum's own parts.''

Tension radiated through Law's neck and shoulders. "Where would he get parts like that?"

"They could have a location where they're kept. Or he could be paying someone to smuggle them out of the company." Andy shrugged. "Although that seems like a lot of trouble to go to for parts he could get elsewhere."

"What else? What other ways could he get his hands on these parts?"

"I suppose Caroline could have had some at her place the night she was kidnapped. The part is made for the types of engines she developed."

Law's shoulders were on fire. "Or someone could be making the incendiary devices for Greely. Someone inside Quantum, using Quantum's parts."

"Who would do something like—" Andy looked at Law and froze. "You know who it is, don't you?"

Law reached for his cell phone. His head throbbed. He punched in the number and waited for Caroline to answer in her lab.

The line rang endlessly.

He prayed he wasn't right. Prayed he wasn't too late. But mostly, he just prayed. Slamming down the receiver, he bolted for the door. He'd take Andy with him, but the genius was in no shape. "Hold down the fort, Dexter. Call Vincent and Whitney and fill them in. Tell them Caroline's lab assistant Sophie is behind this. And tell them I'm on my way."

Chapter Fifteen

Caroline's hand stilled on the doorknob. Darn. The phone had stopped ringing. She didn't know why she was so upset to miss a call. She wasn't expecting anyone to call. A bitter smile twisted her lips. The only call that would be worth dashing back to the lab was a call from Law. One in which he said he'd made a terrible mistake and begged for her forgiveness.

And that wasn't likely to happen. Not while the sun still shone in the sky and the earth still turned on its axis. She slipped the key back in the lock and slid the mechanism home once again. The door secure, she slipped her keys in her purse and turned back to Jimmy. "It was probably Natalie wondering if I'd changed my mind about having dinner at my parents' house."

Jimmy raised his eyebrows. "Do you want to have dinner with your parents? I can drive you up there."

"No. I'll see them tomorrow. And I guess Quint and Natalie are stopping back to pick me up later tonight. Until then I just want to get some work done.

It's been so long. And besides, a late dinner with you and working into the night feels like old times.''

He smiled. ''Some of my favorite memories.''

She settled into step beside Jimmy. Sophie had left only a half hour ago, and it had taken Caroline until now to start to relax. If they didn't find out who was working with Hutch soon, Caroline would have to transfer Sophie to another department. She couldn't work suspecting her assistant was plotting her doom.

When they reached the bank of elevators, they turned and headed down the stairway. Taking the stairs down to the first-floor cafeteria had always been a part of their late-night tradition. A chance to stretch their legs after a long evening of work. And before the long night ahead.

Even with the tension Sophie provided, Caroline had been right to choose a night in the lab over a dinner in Lake Forest. She'd see her parents tomorrow. Tonight was all about returning to normal.

As barren as her life had been before the Solar Sons had kidnapped her, she had enjoyed every moment of her work. In her lab she felt as if she was doing something useful. Something important. She hadn't needed a social life. She hadn't needed love.

A pang registered in her chest. She bit her lip and pushed the sensation away. ''I hope they have something good on the menu tonight.''

''Are you sure you don't want to go to a restaurant instead of the cafeteria?'' Jimmy's eyes flashed with excitement in the darkened stairwell.

Caroline hesitated. She really wanted to settle into her old comfortable routine. Besides, Law had told her not to leave the building until one of the Chicago

Confidential agents came to pick her up. After last night's chase through the rain, the last thing she was going to do was disregard that warning. "I heard they have a new chef downstairs. I'd like to see what he can do."

Jimmy shrugged. "If that's what you want. I wish you would have made this easier." He grabbed her arm and pushed something against her ribs.

She looked down, not wanting to believe her eyes. Jimmy held a gun. A gun pointed right at her. "What are you doing?"

"Don't worry, Caroline. It's going to be all right. Everything is going to be all right. Just come with me."

Shock stuttered through her mind. Jimmy was pointing a gun at her. "Why, Jimmy? What—"

"Don't say any more. I don't want to shoot you. Please don't make me."

They reached the bottom of the stairwell. Still holding the gun on her, Jimmy scanned their identification cards into the lock and pushed the door open. He pulled her out into the night.

Caroline's white lab coat flapped in the stiff wind. Panic raced through her mind. She tried to pull away from Jimmy, but he held her fast. He was stronger than she'd ever guessed.

He pulled her around the corner and into the alley stretching behind the Quantum Building. Dumpsters flanked both sides. A car was stopped up ahead, its headlights bouncing off the concrete walls around them and making her lab coat glow in the night.

"It's all right. Don't worry." Jimmy pulled her forward.

Just as they reached the idling vehicle, a voice reached from behind the glaring lights. "Good work, earth brother."

Caroline froze. A scream caught in her throat. She knew that voice. She'd know it anywhere. She spun around to run.

Jimmy's hand clamped down on her bicep like a vise. Looking into her eyes, he smiled at her, his fondness obvious. "He's going to take you back where you belong, Caroline. He's going to make you one with the earth again. Like you always wanted. Then we can really do the earth's work. Together."

Oh, God! Jimmy was one of the Solar Sons. "Did you give Hutch the key to my apartment?"

"I copied your apartment key in your desk at the lab. Hutch needed a way in. That was the best way. I taped the lock of the back door of your building open, and Hutch used the key to enter your apartment. I didn't want you to get hurt."

"And Mrs. Hansen?"

"I didn't want her to get hurt, either."

"So you sent her the chocolates."

"I remembered you gave her chocolates for Christmas. I thought it would be the easiest way to get her to swallow enough barbiturates to knock her out."

Two shadows moved out from behind the glaring headlights, one hulking, the other thin with a halo of red-gold hair around his head. They walked toward her. The heels of their shoes tapped the pavement and echoed off the tall buildings on either side.

Panic hummed in her ears. "And the firebomb, Jimmy? Hutch injured you. You were burned."

"He wouldn't have been hurt if he'd done as I said." Hutch's voice washed over her.

Her knees sagged like rubber. She hadn't heard his voice since she was in the Solar Sons compound, completely at his mercy. She leaned against Jimmy to stay on her feet.

"Clumsy fool was trying to save you. Isn't that right, brother Jimmy?"

Jimmy looked chagrined. "I had the extinguisher ready. I figured if I bumped the box right before I gave it to you, you wouldn't get burned too badly."

Her stomach rolled. First Jimmy had set her up to be kidnapped, then he'd gone along with Hutch's attempt to turn her into a human torch. "How badly is too badly, Jimmy?"

"It was all for the earth, Caroline. Remember that. You love the earth, too. I thought you would understand. You do understand, don't you?" He stared at her, pleadingly, as if he expected an answer.

Hutch and his henchman stopped. She could see him clearly, even in the shadows. His frizzy red-gold ponytail. His ice-blue eyes. The severe line of his thin lips.

Fear shuddered through her.

Jimmy held her tight. "It's going to be all right, Caroline. Once you're part of the earth for good, Hutch will let you come back to the lab. We'll work together again. You'll see."

She skewered Jimmy with an incredulous look. "And you believe that?"

"Of course. Hutch promised to save you, like he tried to before."

Caroline's head spun. She remembered how Hutch

had tried to save her. She remembered every lie and threat and humiliation. But she had only to look in his shadowed eyes to know that this time saving her was the farthest thing from his mind. "Hutch isn't planning to save me, Jimmy. He's planning to kill me."

"Kill?" Jimmy's eyes grew wide. He glanced from Caroline to Hutch.

Hutch nodded. "Caroline has become an enemy of the earth."

"No." Jimmy shook his head. He focused on Caroline, his eyes pleading. "Tell Hutch how much you love the earth. Tell him how devoted you are to your work. The earth's work. Tell him you'll follow him."

Caroline held her ground, glaring into Hutch's eyes. She didn't feel devotion to the cult leader. She didn't feel guilt. She wouldn't be manipulated by him any longer. "I do love the earth, Jimmy. But Hutch uses the earth to justify murder and destruction. I'll never follow him."

"No." The pitch of Jimmy's voice soared. He turned panicked eyes on Hutch. "She's not an enemy of the earth. I won't let you—"

A small pop echoed off the buildings flanking the alley.

Jimmy slumped against Caroline, his grip on her arm slackening. She struggled to hold him, but couldn't. His limp body fell to the ground.

Caroline looked down at Hutch's hand. He held a gun equipped with a silencer. And it was pointed at her chest. "I've suspected for some time that Jimmy was more devoted to you than to the Solar Sons. We can't have that. It weakens our army. And we need a strong army. Mother Earth deserves to be defended."

Anger rose in Caroline's throat like bile. Jimmy had done horrible things, but he didn't deserve this. He didn't deserve to die. "You bastard."

"I only wish you had been able to purge the evil from your thoughts, Caroline. You would have served the earth well. And I think you would have served me well, too." He raised his free hand and trailed a finger along her jaw and down the tender skin of her neck. "Maybe you still can."

A shudder wracked her body at the thought of his plans for her. His touch made her desperately want to wash. The opposite of Law's touch, so gentle, so loving, so right. Law's touch, Law's love had brought her back from the dead. He'd given her strength. The strength to make her own decisions once again. The strength to choose the life she wanted. The strength to stand on her own two feet. "You're going to have to kill me, Hutch. Because I'd rather die than serve you."

His eyes hardened. His face contorted with rage. "Very well. If you refuse to be useful in the earth's army, then you truly are our enemy. And there's only one thing we do to our enemies. We eliminate them."

Caroline had felt his rage before. She'd heard him utter those words, the order to eliminate the enemy.

And she remembered the night Gordon Doeller had been killed.

She looked down at Jimmy's body, crumpled on the pavement. Memories long buried fought free. Jimmy had been there the night Gordon died. He'd been the one who'd tied Gordon with strips of Gordon's own wool sweater. The same wool sweater given to all the Quantum executives. The wool sweater whose button Hutch had planted in her bedroom as a threat. And when Hutch gave the order to eliminate Gordon Doeller, Jimmy had doused the SUV with gasoline, struck a match and tossed it into the vehicle. "You ordered Jimmy to kill Gordon Doeller."

"Of course I did. He had to prove himself, and Doeller was an enemy. Jimmy was a good soldier once. He carried out orders. Before he started following you around like a puppy. Before you ruined him."

"And you laughed at Gordon's screams. You threw your head back and laughed."

"He was an enemy." Hutch smiled, the expression chilling her to the bone. "I fight for the earth, Caroline. You know that. I love the earth and I will do anything to defend her. Including killing you."

LAW MET VINCENT AND WHITNEY in the lobby of the Quantum Building. Vincent shook his head. "She's not in the lab. Electronic records show she and a Jimmy Flaherty exited the back door."

Alarm jolted Law. He'd thought Hutch's contact at Quantum was Sophie. Could Jimmy be the one setting her up to be kidnapped? Could Jimmy be taking her to Hutch now?

A cold weight settled in the pit of his stomach. It made perfect sense. The package containing the incendiary device would never have to go through security scrutiny if Jimmy assembled it himself in the lab. And Caroline trusted Jimmy like no one else. It would be easy for him to gain her confidence, all the while reporting every detail of her life to Hutch Greely.

The thought chilled him. Of course Caroline wouldn't think twice about leaving the lab with Jimmy. She would feel safe with him. She would never guess Jimmy would deliver her straight into Hutch's hands.

Law forced himself to breathe deeply. He might be assuming the worst. Jimmy might not be Hutch's contact. But he sure as hell wasn't going to take the chance. "When did they leave?"

"They signed out ten minutes ago."

Damn. They could be blocks away by now. "Where is the back door?"

The security guard at the desk pointed. "The one they left from is around the corner to the right. Second door you'll reach on that side."

Law headed out the door at a run. Vincent and Whitney followed. When they reached the door Caroline and Jimmy had used, they stopped.

Law scanned the streets. Lights from neighboring office buildings twinkled in the night. The clank and hiss of Chicago's el train streaked past on tracks two stories overhead. Cars, cabs and limousines swished past on the street.

Caroline had to be around here somewhere, but where? Jimmy could have spirited her off in a cab, taking away any chance of Law finding her before it was too late.

He turned to Vincent. "Did you call in the local cops to help?"

"Already taken care of. I've put an all-points bulletin out for Caroline in addition to the one already out for Hutch Greely."

Law swallowed into a dry throat. Vincent's words should reassure him, but they did nothing of the kind. The only thing that would reassure him was finding Caroline before it was too late.

"Wait." Whitney pointed at a set of headlights glaring past Dumpsters in a side alley.

Law and Vincent flattened themselves against the concrete wall next to Whitney. All three of them slipped their weapons from their shoulder holsters and held them at the ready.

Law could make out only the silhouettes of people in front of the headlights. An innocent discussion in an alley? Not likely. A drug deal? Possibly.

A dark shape lay on the pavement. A body. Law's gut twisted into an even tighter knot. *It couldn't be.*

One of the silhouettes moved. A loose coat flapped around the figure and caught the light. A white lab coat. Blond hair whipped in the wind.

Caroline.

Law nodded to Vincent and Whitney and the three of them advanced, keeping hidden behind the Dumpsters. As they drew closer, the shadows disappeared into the headlights' glare. Law squinted, trying to see.

A hulking figure moved up beside the other two, what looked like a small automatic rifle cradled in his hands. *Pike.* The behemoth leveled his weapon on Caroline.

Law's heart raced. His worst fears had become

reality. Hutch already had Caroline. And if Law, Vincent and Whitney weren't careful, she would be dead with a pull of a trigger.

The skinny shadow Law assumed was Hutch halted, as if he heard something, then nodded to Pike. The big man planted himself in the middle of the alley, facing them, sweeping the shadows with the barrel of his weapon.

Hutch grasped Caroline's arm, pulling her toward the car.

Adrenaline spiked Law's blood. He couldn't let Hutch get into the car with Caroline. It would be virtually impossible to find them once they drove away.

Leveling his Glock, he took a bead on the car's tires. Once he shot, all hell would break loose. But he didn't have a choice. He couldn't let Hutch take Caroline. He glanced at Vincent and Whitney. Both gave him a nod, understanding what he was about to do, ready for the outcome.

Drawing a deep breath, he held the gun steady and squeezed the trigger.

The tires popped one by one, an echo of the gunfire.

"Federal officers," Vincent shouted. "Put your weapons down and your hands on top of your heads."

In answer, Pike squeezed the trigger. Law, Vincent and Whitney ducked back behind the Dumpsters. Lead sprayed the alley and bounced off steel and concrete. The barrage seemed to last for minutes. When it stopped, Law raised his head.

Pike's big form ducked into a door at the mouth of the alley. Hutch and Caroline were nowhere to be seen.

Vincent and Whitney sprang to their feet beside Law. Together the three advanced through the alley, taking turns covering as the others moved forward.

They reached the body lying on the pavement. Jimmy Flaherty's vacant eyes stared into the night. Blood pooled beneath him, staining his lab coat red.

Law stooped to check for a pulse, though he knew it was no use. Jimmy was dead.

And Caroline would be dead, too, unless he found her.

When they reached the door into which Pike disappeared, Whitney peeked into the coffee shop. She gasped. "He has hostages in there. Two teenagers."

"Damn." Vincent plucked his radio off his belt. "We'll need a SWAT team, the works. Whitney, let me know every move he makes."

From his angle, Law couldn't see into the shop. "Are Hutch and Caroline in there, too?" he asked Whitney.

"I don't think so. The place is pretty small. I should be able to see them from here."

Damn. If they weren't inside, then Hutch had her on the streets of Chicago somewhere. All he would have to do was flag down a cab or steal a car and he'd be long gone. "I'm going to go look for them."

He loped off before Vincent had a chance to object. He didn't want to hear it. If he waited for backup, there was an almost certain chance that Hutch would get away. And that meant...

His shoes slapped concrete. He raked the dark

streets with a desperate gaze. Headlights streaked by.
Cars. Taxicabs. Usually it was murder trying to find
a cab in the South Loop at this time of night. But
tonight the streets seemed to be teeming with them.
Hutch could have flagged down any one of them,
forced Caroline inside and whisked her away.

A hollow feeling drilled into the pit of his stomach. Caroline's words after they'd found the Petrol
letter Hutch had left echoed in his memory and ached
in his chest with each breath. He'd been convinced
she would be better off as far away from him as
possible. He'd been wrong.

If he hadn't pulled away from her, she never
would have been with Jimmy tonight. She'd be by
his side. Safe.

Where she belonged.

The thought jolted through him like an electric
charge. He kept moving. He had to concentrate. He
had to find her or none of his impossible fantasies
would matter.

He increased his pace, dodging through the few
people wandering the streets. His heart slammed
against his ribs. His breathing roared in his ears. He
scanned each cab as it passed, coming up empty
every time.

This wasn't working. He couldn't search every cab
in Chicago. Even with Vincent calling for backup
and putting an all-points bulletin out for Hutch and
Caroline, the chances of them being found were dis-
mal. Law had to figure out a better way. He had to
think like Hutch.

He pulled his eyes from the cabs and looked
straight ahead. An el platform loomed in front of him

almost two stories above the streets. If Hutch boarded a train, he could be on the other side of town before the police expanded their search to include more than the surrounding blocks. And no one would expect him to smuggle a hostage aboard the el.

The outlines of a small group of people milled around waiting for the next train. And in that group, Law caught a glimpse of something white flapping in the stiff wind.

Heart leaping, he started up the stairs to the platform. The sound of a train approaching made the steel-and-wood structure tremble. He quickened his pace, taking steps two at a time. He reached the top, ran past the fare vending machines and vaulted a turnstile.

The train rumbled to a stop along the platform. Doors slid open, and the few people waiting climbed aboard. Up ahead, Caroline's white lab coat glowed in the light bathing the platform. Hutch shoved her into one of the cars.

Law came to a dead halt. He could never run the length of the platform before the train pulled out. If he didn't board this train, he'd have to wait for the next one. They could get off at the next platform or transfer trains and he'd have no way of knowing. No way of following. He jumped through the closest door just before it closed.

The train lurched forward. Holding on to steel poles, he stood near the door. The emergency doors at the end of the car only opened from the inside. If he exited the car, he wouldn't be able to get into the next one from the outside. But he would be ready to get off at the next stop and rush to the car where

Hutch held Caroline. He clutched his gun in his hand and held it close to his body, the steel slick in his sweaty palm. The announcement of the next stop drifted over the speaker, muffled and soft like mumbles through cotton batting. The car slowed and stopped. The door slid open.

Law jumped from the car, holding his Glock at the ready. Eyes on the door he'd seen Hutch drag Caroline through, he dodged around a late commuter exiting the el.

A white lab coat flashed in the corner of Law's eye.

Hutch dragged Caroline from the car. She stumbled, landing hard on her knees on the edge of the wooden-plank platform. Hutch yanked her to her feet, pushing the silenced barrel of a gun into her ribs, and looked straight at Law. A bitter smile slithered over Greely's lips. ''No heroics this time, Davies, or she dies.''

Chapter Sixteen

Law's pulse pounded in his ears, louder than the noise of the train pulling away from the platform. He didn't dare make a move, not with Hutch's gun planted in Caroline's ribs. He had to figure out a way to get her away from the cult leader.

Caroline's eyes met Law's. As if soaking up strength from the sight of him, she raised her chin a notch. "Let me go, Hutch. Law is a federal agent. You won't get out of this alive."

Hutch scoffed. "Don't you think I know what he is? Do you think that lessens my dedication to the earth?"

Law thought back to the day in Caroline's lab. The day of the fire. The day he'd told Caroline he was part of Chicago Confidential. "Jimmy told you who I am, didn't he?"

Caroline's lips compressed.

Hutch shook his head. "Jimmy didn't know anything. He just told me about what happened after the fire. How you kept details from Quantum security. How you confessed something to Caroline, something that surprised her. It wasn't hard to figure out the rest.''

"And that's why you cleared out of the compound. You suspected we were on to you.''

"I knew you were planning something. You didn't think that man you sent to infiltrate my compound would fool me, did you? He didn't truly love the earth. I saw it right away. I wasn't about to let you come in and arrest my people. I look out for my followers. The loyal ones, at least.'' He glared down at Caroline. Grasping her by the neck, he poked the gun harder into her ribs.

She gasped for breath.

Anger surged like adrenaline into Law's bloodstream. He took a step forward.

"Back off or I'll shoot.'' Hutch angled Caroline's body between himself and Law.

Law stepped back.

"I knew you wouldn't take the chance. Set the gun down.''

Law gritted his teeth. If he gave up his gun, he'd be defenseless. Both he and Caroline would be at Hutch's mercy. But Hutch was right. He couldn't take the chance Caroline would be hurt. He could never take that chance.

You're hurting me now. Her words from this morning pulsed through his mind.

"Put the gun down, Davies.''

Law stooped and set the gun on the wooden planks of the platform.

"Kick it to me.''

He pushed the gun toward Hutch with a stroke of his foot. It stopped its slide a foot away.

Hutch smiled. Keeping his gaze on Law, he kicked the Glock, sending it clattering off the end of the platform. It landed on the planks beside the tracks, just inches from falling over the edge to the street below.

The sound of a train trembled through the air like approaching doom.

Hutch stepped closer to the tracks, dragging Caroline with him.

She watched Law, her gaze never wavering.

She was the bravest, the strongest woman he knew. Not only had she overcome Hutch's brainwashing, judging from the tilt of her chin, she'd stood up to the cult leader, as well. And now, her life on the line, she stood proud and strong, looking at him with the same love in her eyes he'd seen in bed this morning.

The same love that ached in his heart.

Law opened and closed his fists by his sides. He loved her with all he had to give. But it wasn't enough. Not enough to keep them together, and not enough to save them now.

You're afraid to take the leap.

Was Caroline right? Was he afraid? How could he be afraid in the face of her unshakable courage? How could he be afraid of claiming the woman he loved?

The train rumbled closer, but didn't seem to slow. Hutch inched to the edge of the platform.

Warning blared in Law's mind. Each track carried an electric charge strong enough to severely injure, if not kill, a person. But wood planking formed a narrow walkway between and on either side of the rails. If Hutch jumped onto the wood, he could run down the side of the rails to make his escape. He could also drop Caroline on the tracks on his way.

Law tensed. Whatever the cult leader was planning, he wouldn't get away with it. He wasn't going to hurt Caroline. Nothing would hurt her ever again. Law wouldn't allow it.

The train grew louder, drowning out even the pounding of Law's heart.

Caroline looked into Law's eyes, as if she knew what was coming. As if she trusted him to know, as well.

We belong together.

She gave him a nod.

He leaped at Hutch.

Hutch swung the gun out from behind Caroline, trying to point the barrel at Law before he could cross the expanse between them.

Caroline plowed her elbow into Hutch's stomach.

Hutch doubled over. Still grabbing hold of Caroline's neck, he gasped, the gun shaking in his hand.

Before he could steady his aim, Law chopped down on Hutch's arm.

Hutch cried out. His hand went limp and the gun hit the wood planking and fell onto the tracks. Skittering between the rails, it fell to the street.

Face contorting with anger, Hutch shoved Caroline toward the rails.

Law grabbed her around the waist, preventing her

from falling the few feet to the tracks just as the train streaked by.

Greely's footfalls thundered across the platform. Reaching the end, he swung himself over the edge and lowered himself to the planks on the edge of the tracks.

Law's throat went dry. Greely wasn't running away. He was heading straight for the spot Law's gun had lodged next to the tracks.

Law struggled to his feet and raced after Greely.

He reached the cult leader just as his hand closed around the gun's grip. Law plowed into his back, knocking him to the wooden planks. Law landed on top of him, inches from falling over the edge to the busy street below.

Greely held on to the gun. Bringing it up, he squeezed the trigger.

A shot echoed off the buildings. The bullet went wild, missing Law.

Law grabbed his wrist.

Greely clawed at his fingers. Twisting Law's arm around his body, he leveraged Law off him. He slammed Law's wrist against the edge of the planks. Law's Rolex shattered. The glass face bit into his flesh. The force of the second blow numbed Law's arm. He gritted his teeth and held on.

Suddenly Caroline was beside him, scratching at Hutch's gun hand, digging her fingers into Hutch's eyes.

Hutch's grip loosened.

Law wrenched the gun free.

Scrambling to his knees, Hutch lunged for the gun.

He missed, hurtling over the edge of the planks to the street below. A sickening thud echoed between buildings. Car horns blared. Tires screeched. A second thud shook the air.

Law grasped the edge of the planks and looked down to the street. Cars stopped dead. Headlights illuminated Hutch's still body, facedown on the pavement, his torso pinned under a tire.

Law had seen death before. But he still couldn't stop the shudder that rolled through him.

"Is he…?" Caroline let the question hang in the air, as if she was both hoping for and afraid of the answer.

"Yes. He's dead." Law shoved himself into a sitting position, away from the edge. He couldn't have stopped Hutch's fall. Truth was, he didn't even want to. But such a death was still horrifying.

Caroline's warm hand rested on his shoulder. "It's really over then, isn't it?"

Law grasped her hand and held it to his lips. He kissed her palm, drawing in the scent of her, the feel of her. He met her eyes, almost afraid to breathe. "The nightmare is over. The rest I hope is just beginning."

Her hair whipped around her face. A wrinkle dug between her eyebrows. "The rest?"

"You and me."

She bit her lower lip as if afraid of what he'd say next.

All along he'd tried to keep from hurting her. But by being afraid to let his love for her sweep him away, he'd hurt her terribly. "You were right, Caroline. I was afraid. Afraid to put myself on the line again. Afraid to take a leap of faith.''

Tears welled up in her eyes, making her irises bluer and deeper than Lake Michigan. ''And now?''

''I'm not about to waste my life being afraid. And I'm not about to lose one more second with you.''

A tear broke loose and trickled down one cheek.

''I love you, Caroline. I may never truly deserve you, but I'd like to spend my life trying. If you'll marry me.''

''Of course I will.''

He stood. Straddling a rail, he pulled her into his arms. She felt so good, so right. Like she belonged there. Like she always had.

And now he knew he belonged with her, too. And he'd never let her go. Never again.

Epilogue

"So what do you think of this one, Caroline? A dress
fit for a queen, wouldn't you say?" Kathy pointed a
polished fingernail to a flowing concoction of white
satin and tulle gracing the glossy pages of a magazine featuring designer wedding gowns.

Caroline hesitated. She glanced at Natalie for help.
Her sister pored over another one of the magazines
spread out on Kathy's desk, conducting her own
search for the perfect dress.

Sighing, Caroline turned back to the dress Kathy
had found. The dress was fit for a queen, no question
about it. The only problem was, Caroline was no
queen. She didn't even want to pretend she was one.
She had worked too hard to be exactly who she was.
And now she had the perfect life. A challenging job,
a husband-to-be that she adored and who adored her,
and a future that was open for the choosing. She
didn't need to pretend anything.

Raising her eyes from the magazines, she met
Law's gaze from across the Solutions lobby.

He smiled, mirroring the look of pure joy and con-
tentment she knew radiated from her own face. Law

was as happy as she was. And once Chicago Confidential's case involving the oil companies was resolved and he was able to quit his job with Petrol, they would set about building a happy home and a family of their own.

"Well?" Kathy prompted. "What about the dress?"

Caroline shrugged. "Maybe we'll just elope."

Natalie snapped her own magazine shut and rolled her eyes. "Maybe Quint and I will join you. Our parents would love that."

Caroline flinched at the thought of disappointing her parents. They'd been so wonderful since the night she and Law had gone to Lake Forest for dinner, shortly after Hutch had fallen to his death. They'd accepted Law immediately. They hadn't pressured her. They'd just supported her and loved her and taken her back into the Van Buren fold, no questions asked. Just the way Natalie had. "I suppose we'd better give Mom and Dad the big society weddings they deserve."

"Two weddings a week apart. It'll be half a month of nonstop merriment and networking at the Van Buren household," Natalie said with a chuckle, her smile wider than Caroline had ever seen it. Of course, that smile had everything to do with her own fiancé, Quint Crawford, who stood across the lobby talking business with Law, Vincent, Whitney and a nearly recovered Andy. Slowly they disappeared down the hall leading to the boardroom.

Chicago Confidential had done a splendid job of bringing an end to the terrorism of the Solar Sons. Not only had Law saved her from Hutch, but Vincent and Whitney had subdued Pike without any of the hostages getting hurt.

Thank God it was all over.

She still felt sad about Jimmy. About how Hutch had used and manipulated him, about how she'd blocked his involvement from her mind, and mostly about Sophie who had been red-eyed and depressed since Jimmy's death. The only good that had come of it was that she and Sophie had forged an understanding. While they would probably never become best friends, at least they could work together.

Kathy flipped through the photos until she landed on another luxurious gown. "How about this one?"

"Well…" Caroline searched for the right words. "I don't think it's quite me."

Outside in the hall, the elevator bell dinged.

Kathy circled her desk. "Hold that place. We'll find a dress for you yet, Caroline."

Caroline almost sighed with relief. Saved by the bell. At least for a few minutes.

The glass doors swung open, and six feet of tall, dark and regal strode into the room. The man was handsome, as well. Movie-star handsome. Black hair curled around the collar of his Armani suit. His dark gaze raked the room.

Kathy looked up at the visitor. "It's nice to see you, Prince Jav— ah, Zahir."

The prince bowed to Kathy, and then to Caroline and Natalie, as well.

A door opened in the rear of the lobby and Law emerged from the direction of the boardroom. "Javid, it's good to see you."

Dark eyes shifted back to Caroline and Natalie.

Law circled an arm around Caroline's waist and pulled her close for a quick hug.

She leaned into him, despite the guest looking at her with suspicious eyes.

Law chuckled. "This is Caroline and Natalie Van Buren. You have nothing to worry about with them."

The prince's jaw relaxed slightly. "Nice to meet you." His voice was as distinct as his appearance. The best Caroline could tell, it was a mix of northeastern United States and Middle Eastern, both crisp and mellow at once.

"Caroline and I are getting married. So are Natalie and Quint."

"We have something in common, then."

"Yes, I heard you were getting married, as well," Law said. "Or at least your undercover persona was getting married. In fact, that's why Vincent asked you here."

"That is what I assumed."

"Well, if you'll follow me, everyone is waiting in the special-ops room. And after the meeting, Quint and I can give you some advice about choosing a tux." Law gave Caroline a wink and slipped his arm from around her waist.

She watched Law and the prince walk across the lobby. The way Law looked at her, she could wear rags to her wedding and still feel like a queen. And that was all she needed. As long as they both shall live.

*   *   *   *   *

And the story continues....
Next month don't miss
the final exciting installment of
CHICAGO CONFIDENTIAL:
PRINCE UNDER COVER
by Adrianne Lee
Turn the page for a sneak peek!

Chapter One

The chauffeur helped Lina into the back seat, then turned to Miah. "Ms. Mohairbi, I found this on the floorboard. I thought perhaps it had fallen out of your pocketbook."

Miah frowned, accepting the envelope. The moment she recognized the block lettering, she froze. This hadn't come from her purse. Someone had placed it in the car. When? How? "Did you leave the limousine unattended at any time, Mehemet?"

His black eyes became evasive. "Only one moment...to answer nature. But I lock first."

"Okay." It was a silly thing to lie about, but she knew he couldn't have locked the car. Otherwise the note would not have been in it. And it was unlikely he'd seen whomever had put the envelope inside it. She quickly read the enclosed note, feeling the heat drain from her cheeks. Miah squished the blackmail note in her fist and shoved it into her pocket.

Miah squelched the urge to curse and ducked into the car, letting the soft leather embrace her. She'd thought the first payment to the vile extortionist would be the end of it. But there had been a second

demand. And now another. God, how naive she'd
been. He wanted ten thousand more or he'd ruin her
wedding. Destroy her mother. Start a scandal that
could strip her of her future. She stared out the window as the limo merged with traffic. She hated the
shivering in her stomach that felt as if she'd swallowed a full glass of ice shavings.

Fear.

Truth didn't scare Miah. Lies did.

Perhaps that was because she'd discovered last
January that her whole life had been a lie.

"Darling, is something wrong?" Lina touched her
clasped hands. "You're very pale. For a moment
there, you looked absolutely terrified."

"Terrified? Don't be silly. No, no," she managed
in a tone that sounded normal. "I was thinking about
the wedding. Nothing for you to fret about, honest."

But her mother's brow knit, a sign she wasn't going to let this go so easily. "Are you having second
thoughts about marrying someone you've been betrothed to since you were a baby?"

She doubted anyone would blame her if she was
having second thoughts, but she couldn't afford
them. She had agreed to the marriage without coer-
cion from anyone, agreed to it for all that it would
give her—including her own money, an enormous
inheritance that would allow her to pay off the extortionist, once and for all. She said, "No second
thoughts."

None she would admit to out loud anyway. Not to
her mother. Not to herself.

The limousine pulled up to their building farther

along Lake Shore Drive. They occupied a penthouse with a magnificent view of Lake Michigan. It was a far cry from the tenement apartment they'd called home for most of her life.

Miah walked Lina through the lobby to their private elevator. "I'm just going to change into something a little more comfortable."

"MORE COMFORTABLE" was impossible for Miah to achieve. The ice chips in her stomach still had her shivery half an hour later. She caught a glimpse of her reflection in the glass doors as she exited the apartment complex. Her long, lean legs flashed from beneath the scrap of hot-pink skirt that hugged her slim hips, while her slender upper body sported a neon-green, sheer top over a creamy camisole. Her thick, blunt-cut raven hair swung across the middle of her back and shoulders with every step, and framed her face...which looked a shade too pale at the moment.

Her outfit drew a look of disapproval from the chauffeur as she met him at the curb. She climbed into the back seat of the limo and waited until he closed the door, then tugged on the hem of her short skirt. Her mother had tried leaning her toward the conservative styles *she* favored, but Miah needed variety. Color. Flash.

Making her clothing allowance stretch had meant shopping in consignment stores and thrift shops. Even though she could now afford to buy her favorite designers new, or spend thousands on a single blouse, she still shopped in the same stores she'd always frequented.

She liked *her* style. But no one else seemed to. Not her mother, not her newly discovered father, and especially not her fiancé. Too bad, she had decided. She was who she was. *Nothing* could change that. And today, she needed the "old" Miah more than ever to get through the next few hours.

She realized that she was so tense, a light breeze could probably blow her over. She needed some TLC. Needed Cailin. Her best friend. Needed a tall thirst-quenching beer. Needed one last afternoon to be the woman she'd been pre-January. Tomorrow, her life would change forever. Today, she could indulge in some of her favorite things, could forget a blackmailer's demands. His threats. Could bank the fires of worry about her mother. Stave off the apprehension she felt about the marriage.

She instructed Mehemet to leave her at Finnigan's Rainbow—a family-owned-and-operated bar and grill—on Michigan Avenue in the heart of the shopping district, and take the rest of the day off.

Cailin was working the bar with her brother, Rory. He grinned at Miah and hollered above the din, "Princess, what brings you slumming on the eve of your wedding?"

Princess. Miah slid onto a bar stool. She had to admit that aside from the money for her mother, the fact that she would be an honest-to-God princess after saying "I do" touched a chord inside her, as though something internal had aligned, connected.

Cailin snapped her brother's backside with a bar

towel. "She's not officially a princess until tomorrow, you doof."

The Finnigans all had fiery red hair and mischievous blue eyes. Cailin was the only girl, a natural beauty. She greeted Miah with a smile. "Hey, girlfriend, nice to see you looking like your old self."

"Thanks." Miah caught her friend's gaze darting to the door. Bobby "The Buzzard" Redwing, Cailin's ex-boyfriend, had been hassling her. Miah had no more interest in encountering The Buzzard than Cailin; he was a reporter for the very tabloid she feared the blackmailer would sell his story to.

She drew a shaky breath. She had to lose this mood. Quit thinking about the blackmailer. Determined to do just that, she forced a smile. "Hey, Rory, can 'almost royalty' get an ice-cold one and a slice of pizza in this dive?"

Cailin laughed while Rory set a frosted mug of foaming beer before Miah, then went to fetch her pizza, leaving Miah and Cailin to chat. But the first thing out of Cailin's mouth was, "Uh-oh."

Her gaze fixed on something over Miah's shoulder.

Miah tensed. "Is it 'The Buzzard'?"

"Nope. This one's all yours. *The Gorgeous One.*"

Miah's heart thumped. Talk about stress inducing. He would not be happy to see her dressed like this. She gathered her poise and glanced around at her fiancé. Six feet of gorgeous male animal, the most handsome man she'd ever encountered. Hollywood should have come knocking on his door years ago. Prince Zahir Haji Haleem. His dark, heated gaze

landed on her like a sensual stroke playing over her
body. There was something possessive in that look,
something that sent heat into her belly and fire
through her blood.

She swallowed hard against the knot forming in
her throat. It scared her, this heat she felt every time
he was near. If his look, his casual touch could make
her this flustered, this hot, he might just burn her up
during serious intimacy. And she didn't doubt for a
minute that this man would be more than proficient
at lovemaking.

She took a swig of the beer, then thumped the mug
onto the bar, slipped off the stool and, with her three-
inch sandals clicking on the hardwood floor, crossed
to where he waited, as though he'd sent her a silent
command to come to him.

"Hello, Zahir."

"Miah." His gaze did a lazy climb from her gaily
painted toenails, up the strappy pumps and skimpy
clothing, to her face.

She clenched her hands against the blush his sexy
perusal brought to her flesh, lifted her chin and stared
him in the eye. "Like what you see?"

He smirked. "Every man in the bar seems to."

"And you object to that?"

"I believe objections, were I to have any, would
fall on deaf ears." He wore a black, Armani three-
piece suit. His raven hair curled against the virgin-
white of his shirt collar. He smelled of a spicy au-
tumn afternoon, and seemed somehow able to defy
the heat.

"I like color," she said. If he had his way, she'd

be covered from head to toe in flowing veils all fit
for a funeral. But that she would never do.

"Color likes you back." He caught her chin in his
big hand, startling her.

The blush swept her body again, gaining heat this
time as it reached her face. She could pull away, but
sensed the room watching them. She whispered,
"What are you doing?"

He leaned near, as though to kiss her. Her breath
jammed in her throat at the raw sexuality in his very
touch, his very nearness. The pad of his thumb traced
the soft flesh above her upper lip. "Foam…from the
beer."

"Tha-thank you." She took a faltering step back.
"How did you know to find me here, Zahir?"

"Actually, I wasn't looking for you, love." His
voice was a mix of northeastern crisp and Middle
Eastern mellow. "I had no idea you were here. I was
passing by and spotted that tabloid reporter, what's
his name, Redwing, outside." He glanced at the door
as though he half expected The Buzzard to burst
through it, camera flashing. "The last thing I want
is him getting wind of where and when the wedding
is coming down."

Coming down? That was a strange was to refer to
their wedding. She lowered her voice, "Bobby Redwing has been hassling Cailin. He's probably not after you or me."

"In the past, he's been very persistent, very good
at ferreting out…secrets," Zahir said in a distracted
voice as though he were speaking to himself. Then,
he seemed to shake himself and flashed her a too-

quick, too-bright grin. "*You* don't have anything to hide, do you, love?"

Miah flinched. "No. Nothing."

Nothing except a blackmailer's secret.

"What about you, Zahir?" *What don't I know about you?*

His gaze flicked away from hers, a sure sign he *was* hiding something. Miah felt the uneasiness returning, the second-guessing. She was marrying a man she didn't know. A stranger. Who could have secrets she didn't even suspect.

Maybe, *dangerous* secrets.

JAVID BLEW OUT a taut breath and stepped from the dark interior of Finnigan's Rainbow into the blinding afternoon on Michigan Avenue. Pretending to be Zahir was taking its toll. He hated lying, even necessary lying. Just now, he'd have sworn Miah knew, sworn she was going to expose him right there in the pub.

Tomorrow. It would all be over tomorrow. Thank God. He'd survived more than one tight situation in recent days, but none that had left him this rattled…and that was *her* fault.

Heat sizzled off the sidewalk, several degrees cooler than the fire in his belly, a fire for a woman he didn't want to want, a woman he wanted so badly he ached. He took long strides away from the pub, berating himself with every step, unable to abolish the image of her long luscious legs in that scrap of hot-pink, her shapely feet in those high-heeled, mind-numbing sandals, the way that green top made her amber eyes shimmer like spun gold.

"Damn it all." *Miah Mohairbi was an assignment. The daughter of the devil himself.* She was also a vixen. He'd never met a woman quite her equal, and he'd met a lot of women since he'd been old enough to pay attention to his hormones, women here and in the Middle East, women at Harvard during college, women around the globe, at each stop on his worldwide travels as Anbar's goodwill ambassador.

Miah was unique. Beautiful, yes, but she was so much more than that. She had a sharp mind, a wicked tongue, style and defiance. She could be hard one moment, tender the next. To his chagrin, he found the conflicting aspects of her personality endlessly intriguing. If only circumstances were different. If only she were not Sheikh Khalaf Al-Sayed's blood child.

Thank God this torment ended tomorrow. After that, he could guarantee Miah would hate him—once she discovered he'd been lying to her, posing as his twin, once he helped arrest the father she seemed to adore, once he exposed Al-Sayed to the world for the heartless bastard he was.

An odd tightness twisted his heart at the thought of breaking hers.

HARLEQUIN®
INTRIGUE®

**brings you a new miniseries from
award-winning author**

AIMÉE THURLO

**Modern-day Navajo warriors, powerful,
gorgeous and deadly when necessary—these
secret agents are identified only by the...**

Sign
of the
Gray
Wolf

In the Four Corners area of New Mexico, the elite investigators
of the Gray Wolf Pack took cases the local police couldn't—
or wouldn't—accept. Two Navajo loners, known by the code
names Lightning and Silentman, were among the best of the
best. Now their skills will be tested as never before when
they face the toughest assignments of their careers. Read
their stories this fall in a special two-book companion series.

WHEN LIGHTNING STRIKES
September 2002
NAVAJO JUSTICE
October 2002

Available at your favorite retail outlet.

HARLEQUIN®
Makes any time special ®

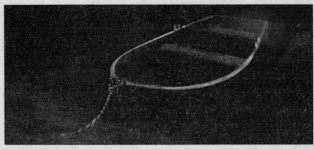